Arthur Pax:

Liquid Dreams

Tim Schafer

ARTHUR PAX: LIQUID DREAMS
Copyright ©2023 Line By Lion Publications
www.pixelandpen.studio
ISBN 9781948807388

Cover Design by Thomas Lamkin Jr.
Editing by Dani J. Caile

To my parents and my Otters: I love you more than you can know. However, this book is for my kids: Klarissa, Seth, Timothy, Sarah, Jackson, Orion, and Paige.

Prologue

Early April, sometime in the late 1400s, Novgorod, Russia

RUSALKA[1] opened her eyes as the sun was still waiting to awaken much like two of her sisters slumbering in their shared bed. It must have been her older sister coming to bed that awoke her. The hut she shared with her three sisters was still shrouded in the purple darkness of the predawn light. She stretched her limbs to shake the sleep out and try to warm them a bit. This past winter was a difficult one, due to the intensity of the wind and the length. Her sister, Snegurochka[2], had been working tirelessly for the past several years. Snegurochka was throwing another one of her tantrums and that meant the winter would be more harsh, for she was the Snow Maiden.

However, today was Rusalka's day and she needed to be fully awake for the task ahead of her. After the long night, Rusalka's stomach rumbled loud enough to stir her slumbering sisters. She wrapped herself in a thick house robe that kept out the chill rolling around the floor to go to the kitchen to gather some food. She found half a loaf of bread baked from yestermorning, a chunk of cheese from the stores and a pat of sweet cream butter to give the bread flavor. She considered that sufficient for the day, but still needed to break the fast. Searching the cluttered table, she located the oat sack, some fresh cream and a jar with some tart seaberries. That would make a good hearty porridge and she went quietly about boiling water to make her small meal.

---

[1]Rusalka; Pronounced: roo-SAL-kah Cyrillic; русалка

[2] Snegurochka; Pronounced: snyeg-oo-ROACH-ka, Cyrillic: Снегу́рочка

One of her three sisters, Zvezda Vechernyaya[3], came in through the door, letting a hint of chill into the cozy house. She was pale with silver hair that shone in the darkened hut. She looked old and young at the same time. Her eyes twinkled with mischief as she saw Rusalka in the kitchen spooning the hot porridge into a wooden bowl and darted to give her a long overdue embrace. Rusalka put her bowl down and shushed Vechernyaya, not wanting to wake the other two sisters. After a quiet embrace she wordlessly asked Vechernyaya if she wanted some of the fresh meal, which Vechernyaya nodded emphatically. They ate while whispering to each other too low for anyone else to hear what the conversation was about, but there was much giggling involved.

After their repast, weary from her night of working in the stables, Vechernyaya changed from her work clothes that consisted of a thick pair of breeches, a roughspun tunic and her reindeer lined hard soled boots all of her clothes were in shades of dark blues and violet. She hated stripping off her warm clothes to put on the chilly bed robes and quickly crawled in bed with the remaining two sisters. As she dropped off to a quick sleep, the youngest looking of the three, and twin to Vechernyaya, sat up in their bed positively beaming.

Zvezda Danica's[4] bright red hair blazed in the dying embers of the fireplace. She looked around the room with her pale blue eyes, settling them on her sisters as they softly snored in the Somniac Land of Nod. She gave a loving smile to each and placed a gentle hand on their faces before rising. She splashed a little cold water on her face and quickly changed from her warm night robe into a pair of breeches and tunic. The style matched Vechernyaya's clothes that were hanging on the wall nearby. However, instead of the cool blues and greys of her sister's clothes, Danica's were warm in shades of red and yellow. They

---

[3] Zvezda Vechernyaya; Pronounced: zuhves-dah vye-CHAIR-nyah-yah, Cyrillic: звезда вечерняя

[4] Zvezda Danica; pronunciation: zuhves-dah dah-NEE-kah Cyrillic: звезда даника

were just as chilly as her sister's bed robes. She quickly braided her unruly hair, then she sat on the bench at the end of the bed and slipped on her reindeer fur lined boots. Seeing the activity in the kitchen, she arose from her seat and went to gather her own food for the day. Snegurochka continued to sleep soundly. She constantly complained about being cold, she snuggled closer to Vechernyaya feeling the loss of warmth that Danica offered.

Rusalka and Danica gathered up in a hug, bid a silent good day to the other and went about their morning rituals. The younger rosy colored one opened the door and skipped out into the darkness. As she stepped outside, a bit of light spread across the horizon. Another day was starting. The evening star had gone to sleep and dawn was waking up the world.

With a sigh, Rusalka gathered her courage to face the cold day. However, this was a day for her, she would be very busy over the next several months. She woke up when her sister Snegurochka went to sleep. They could only be awake opposite each other. One for the warmer months, one for the colder months. For she was Rusalka, a water spirit and the bringer of rains to help fertilize crops for the people who worshipped her.

Rusalka dipped her flowing robes into the nearby river to bring the rains every spring to help soften the ground to help farmers plant their crops. Then after the farmers had tilled and planted she dipped her robes again to bring the soft rains to awaken the sleeping seeds. This is how it was, is, and always will be.

The sisters do not remember a mother or father, they just always have been alive. They have seen countless years come and go, each doing their important jobs for the people of the world. The Zvezdas tend to the stable of their uncles Dazhbog[5] (the embodiment of the sun) and Yutrobog[6] (the embodiment of the moon).

---

[5] Dazhbog; pronunciation: DAHZH-bog, Cyrillic: Дажьбогъ

[6] Yutrobog; pronunciation: YOU-troh-bog, Cyrillic: ютробогъ

Each morning, Danica steps out to harness Dazhbog's roan stallion to his sledge and opens the gate to let the sun ride across the sky, while unharnessing and tending to Yutrobog's pale mare. Each evening, Vyechernaya does the same, but in reverse. It is a tireless job and the sisters barely see each other. Sometimes, when Dazhbog and Yutrobog share the sky together the sisters catch up with each other. Whether it is when they can be seen in the full light of day or in the secrecy of night the sisters always have time for gossip about their uncles, the towns folk, who the new lovers were and anyone who was caught being a rascal.

Rusalka grabbed her flowing robe from the hook next to the door before stepping out of the hut. Shades of grey and blue, the robe's volume held many pleats to trap as much water as possible. She could not catch a cold because she revelled in the water, she was water incarnate. She loved lounging in the river during her time off but that would come later. First, she had a job to do.

She opened the door to go outside and breathed in the fresh smell of the harvest to come. The loamy, earthy smell of undiscovered plants tickled her nose. As she started her day, she heard Danica tending to the horses. The soft wickers of the two lovers made Rusalka smile. *Mayhaps this year they will foal another*, she thought to herself. She wandered about the hut a bit, looking around.

It had been many months since she had been out of the hut and wanted to familiarize herself again with their humble dwelling. The sturdy wooden walls seemed to be made of one piece of wood, the way they all flowed together. Oval and short, it sat in the remains of Snegurochka's snow piles. The thatched roof was just high enough to be out of reach without help. It looked like a few spots were starting to look bare. They had some servants to tend to that, though. Their servants were well treated and in turn, they made sure the sisters were comfortable in their slumber.

"Time to go to work," were the only words she uttered aloud since waking up. Rusalka gathered up her robes, walked purposefully to the nearby river and waded into the frost-touched waters. To someone wandering nearby, they might find this a shock, especially if they did not know her. Seeing a porcelain skinned, grey haired beauty with eyes the color of the promise of a storm wearing thick, flowing, grey and blue robes is one thing. However, watching her walk into a river barely above the freezing point would give anyone a start. However she waded in calmly and as soon as she was satisfied that her robes could not hold any more water, she jumped into the sky. Soaring among the chilled clouds, Rusalka let her bountiful robes seed the clouds with more water, which started a downpour everywhere she flew. Her laughter became thunderous, her smile flashed with electricity. This is what she was born to do. Her heart filled with glee with every drop spilled.

Rusalka brought the rain.

Chapter One

Leprechauns Are People Too

November 15, 2014; Indianapolis

IT was close to two in the afternoon on the 15th of November. I know because it said so on my cell phone. Last night was a bit of a blur between the joint birthday party between myself and my best friend Charles "Chuck" Silver and fighting the forces of evil, i.e. talking to my ex-wife. That woman just really knows when is the absolute worst time to call and complain about something. I was already into my fourth gin and tonic and had my guard down for a bit when she called. We hit up a couple seedy strip clubs to have his birthday licks in for the year and were already in our favorite hole in the wall pub, Rackham's Respite, for the rest of the night. It's not every day that you and your brother-in-arms turn forty one.

Sidebar: You don't know birthday spankings until you've had about eight different strippers give you swats from an old-school paddle. You know, the kind they outlawed in the early '80s. Everyone at one point or another felt the sting from those bastards, whether it was school or home. I hated them as a kid, but get a couple shots of Wild Turkey in your tum-tum, put on some Def Leppard and those strippers could practically do what they wanted with that paddle. Chuck was also a bit of a BDSM junkie. Okay, when I say a bit, I mean, he's into the lifestyle. He has a Domme that calls in on him regularly. If he doesn't get dominated at least once a week, he's a very grumpy boy. What can I say, he's my best friend; I let him talk me into birthday licks once a year. But I digress.

My ex decided to call me when I was feeling pretty good and not paying attention to the number on the screen. You would think that I would have her number saved to avoid her, but you would be wrong. I felt the buzz in my jeans, pulled out my phone and unlocked it without a second thought. After her shrill, harpy-like voice came across the ear piece, I was stuck listening to her alternate between how good we were together and how much she loathed me. It was a pretty short conversation compared to past calls. Well, conversation is pushing it, it was more like a lecture on the sins of my past. Thank god Chuck took the phone from my ear and started barking at her. Not even metaphorically, literally barking at her like a dog. I heard her swear obscenities at him before he cordially bid her a good day and hung up.

My Friend Chuck™ and I were almost inseparable by fate from the day we were born, not exactly by choice. We were born on the same day, just a couple of minutes apart. We were next to each other in the hospital baby ward until our respected parents were able to take us home. We lived a couple of streets over from each other but went to two different elementary schools because of zoning. I mean, I'd seen him around at the local community centers and parks, but we didn't really play together. It wasn't until college that we shared the same space for more than just a few minutes. In fact, we were college roommates at Indiana University in Bloomington, Indiana. We bonded over women, Star Wars, Dungeons and Dragons, and hating frat boys. It was as if I found my hetero life partner. It's not that I'm homophobic, I mean if I were into guys, he would be my type. He stood at a solid 6 feet tall with black hair, blue eyes, a chiseled jawline, an athletic build, and a permanent five o'clock shadow; whereas I stand about 5'9", overweight by about eighty pounds, glasses, a full red beard, and brown hair with the first touch of silver at the temples.

I mean, it's not that we didn't give it the good old college try.

There was a party we went to. The theme of the night was "Renaissance Faire," the kegs needed to be emptied because it was right before the end of the semester and we were plastered. It was about midnight, he had been hitting on pretty much anyone and everyone and I said to myself, "What the hell?" We were laughing and having a good time. I noticed he kept looking at my lips with a quiet desperation in his eyes, as if he were wondering what would happen if we crossed that line. I grabbed him at the base of his neck and leaned in. A spark jumped between our lips and it was on. Our mouths parted only to be joined as one, lips grinding together, tongues probing the inner moistness of our oral cavities. We didn't care what the rest of the attendees thought, it was our time. A soft groan stirred from his chest as the fervor increased. Teeth clashing, hair pulling, he grabbed my butt. I put my all into it. However when our lips and souls parted, I knew I was completely straight. I had nothing going on in the nether regions and neither had he. Later he told me it wasn't that he didn't enjoy it, it was just too vanilla for him. So, we left the party with different people and worked out our sexual frustrations with willing partners.

It took me a few seconds to pull myself out of my mnemonic trip to realize he was talking to me.

"…and Artie, you have got to either save or block her number," Chuck griped. "She's going to just keep doing this to you…" His voice droned on like an adult on Charlie Brown. As I started to sink into a deep funk that I only saw my way out of by the time I reached the bottom of a bottle of gin. The rest of the night was a blur. I know Chuck called a driving service of some kind, which I did NOT expel my ginner demons in. Heh. Get it. Inner demons but with a "G"…that's a good joke. I should write it down.

I remember being transported to my house near Garfield Park with My Friend Chuck™ accompanied by a pregnant, midget hooker named Champagne. I'm sorry. That was insensitive and downright non-PC of me. She was a childbearing, sex-positive working midget. Anywho, they dumped me on my bed and it was nighty-night time.

I don't normally get as drunk as I was, but dammit, I needed to blow off some steam. My job is very stressful and my ex just royally pisses me off, hence the "ex" part of wife. I'm just glad we never had any children. Mostly that was my fault. I am a Believer and bringing kids into that life is kind of difficult. When I say I'm a Believer, it's not in a The Monkees kind of way. I mean I used to think that love was only true in fairy tales, then I met Char. I am a member of a group of people called the Believers in the Mystical Arts and Alchemical Sciences. I'll get more into that later, first you need to know about Char.

Char was short for Charlene, but she hated that name. It reminded her of some old lady that smelled of some long forgotten Avon perfume and had those little strawberry candies in her purse. You know the ones, hard on the outside and a weird liquid center. No one knows where you buy them, believe me, I've looked. I think it just comes with old lady purses. You turn 63 and BOOM, you have a purse that has a small gateway to some kind of confectioner's hell where they are forced to churn out the crunchy, but sickly sweet imitation strawberry flavored treats. It was probably some kind of punishment they deserved, if there was punishment in the afterlife.

Char was 5'5" or so, with multi-hued hair that she colored regularly, a smile that twisted with a wicked sense of humor, and a body to die for. One time a guy almost walked in front of a bus he was so distracted watching her walk down the street, the misogynistic pig. Yes, that guy was me (oink, oink) and I'm fine, thank you for asking. I somehow managed to jump myself back onto the curb as the bus whistled by and the driver blared his horn to remind me that he was there. Just from this event, I should have known she was trouble from the very beginning. She must have seen how I miraculously jumped back to the curb. It felt like an invisible gorilla grabbed me by my overcoat, sweeping me out of harm's way as the bus screamed past my face. That kind of thing leaves an impression. I'm not sure if it was my full red beard, silvering hair or my big tum-tum, but something caught her eye and she crossed the street to check up on me. I was dumbfounded, speechless, and utterly in full mating season lust. No one goes out of their way to help out a stranger in Indianapolis, but here she was.

A casual dalliance with drinks and dinner moved to a full blown relationship in the matter of a few weeks. And the relations... well, a gentleman never tells. Good thing I'm no gentleman. She was a wildcat in bed. Not like a pornstar, because that shit is all camera angles, out-takes, and lots of lube. Nah, she was the real deal. She once did this move that was kind of like a reverse cowgirl, but she was wearing a corset and a pair of fairy wings. I'm not sure exactly how she did it, but she was able to bend over backwards and touch her toes to her ears. Holy clamp, Batman. When she was ready to blow, you just held on for dear life or got left in the wet spot. Wildcat!

Our time was altogether too short, but her entire demeanor changed after we did the civil ceremony. We only had her parents, my mom and My Friend Chuck™. It was a small ceremony, but full of love and beauty. We promised all the normal things, but I didn't promise to be her verbal punching bag. I know it's kind of taboo to talk about male spousal abuse, but I've lived through it and it sucks.

We lasted for almost three years, but it got to be too much and I split. It was exhausting being berated each and every day for tiny things. I made sure to take care of the big stuff, birthdays, holidays, anniversaries: but it was the little stuff, like turning on the wrong burner and melting a plastic mixing bowl that would set her off. And it wasn't long after the verbal abuse that the mental abuse started. The name calling, the constant emasculating remarks she made about how much of a 'girl' I acted like when I wanted to talk about what was bothering me; only made way for her to throw things at me. It was a short jump from throwing things to physically hitting me. Maybe she could have helped with the dishes or her not using me as a way to get her frustrations out; but I'm sure you're not here to listen to me gripe. You want to hear more about the magic stuff. We will get to that. You just need context and that male spousal abuse is a thing that is out there, but because of how it is viewed, it is not as prevalent as female spousal abuse.

Back to the 15th, my head was pounding. Not because of a headache, but because someone was pounding on my door and in my little house, it reverberated everywhere. I believed in living a bachelor slash spartan lifestyle. No pets, no kids, lots of takeout containers, a huge ass TV with the latest gaming system plugged in, and a full bar. I didn't need much else. Another round of pounding on the door finally got me to drag myself to an upright position.

"Yeah, yeah, yeah. I'm coming," I yelled at the persistent portal pugilist. I pulled my pants up, because at some point I must have used the restroom, my fly was undone. I just hope I made it to the toilet and not the oven. Again. The visitor started banging for the umteenth time and in the middle of the third bang, I flung open the door. A very short red-headed man stood there. He was smoking a pipe and wearing a dark green overcoat, which was a regular jacket on full size people. His comically orange hair fluffed out from under a classic, black bowler.

"YE OWE ME FER LAST NIGHT!" he shouted at the top of his lungs in a thick Irish brogue, which was surprisingly loud for a vertically challenged chain smoker.

"Oh, hey Dec," I sighed, "what the hell are you talking about? I don't remember much about last night, much less who I saw." Declan Callum Shaughnessy-Gonzales was your typical looking leprechaun. Short, red haired, always pissed off at someone about something, and smoking like a chimney in the middle of winter.

"You very well know, ya bastard. I saw you with me girl," he huffed. "She went into yer house and was gone fer quite a bit."

I had to focus a bit on what he was implying. Terrible thing is I couldn't remember who his girl was this week. "Which one is this?"

"YE DAMN WELL KNOW! 'Tis the true love of me life, the pear of me eye, the womb I call home, and me business partner." His eyes got all glassy as he teared up thinking about, well, whoever it was.

Then it hit me. "Champagne?"

"DAMN SKIPPY, CHAMPAGNE!!! Ye did the deed, she licked yer tadger and ye tiddy-diddled her in the fud until yer gammy baws spilt in her gash! She didna get her pay and ye are gonna give me wha's due!" as he slipped into a full blown Scottish mouthful. I really hate it when he can't stay in character.

"Your accent is slipping, Dec." I scoffed. His face turned red and he opened his mouth to really let me have it, but deflated.

In a completely "normal" Indiana accent, he looked me in the eye and said, "Did you believe me at least for a little bit? I was trying to live up to the stereotype, homes, but for reals, did you sleep with Champagne? If so, you kind of owe me, being a responsible john and all."

"Bruh. I was so wasted from my birthday bash and dealing with Psycho Char, I passed the fuck out. If she didn't come out for a while, talk to Chuck. He might know what's up. He is into that kinky shit Champagne is known for." I yawned and scratched my ass, because well, it itched. "Come in if you're coming in, Dec. I need to tae a pisser tha'll drown a fish." (in a beautifully perfect Scottish accent), "and don't fucking touch my shoes." Leprechauns are known to have real bad shoe fetishes, like getting off from sniffing a stinky pair of pumps bad. I shuffled off to relieve myself while Declan closed the door and made himself comfortable on the couch, turning on the TV and system.

I heard the first strains of him booting up his favorite game and I yelled, "God, not that fucking duck game again." He had a penchant for playing this game that was a dick of a duck that terrorized a small Dutch village. It was a very niche market and he loved it. I heard him giggling maniacally as I flushed the commode and shuffled into the kitchen to grab some water and a couple of Hangover Miracle Pills™. It was mostly natural herbs and a bit of this and that; but with a couple of these babies, I've never suffered ill effects from a night of drunken shenanigans.

I went back to my room, sniffed a couple of shirts to find one that wasn't too funky, made a mental note to do laundry and headed back out to the living room. I took a moment to reflect on the past 40 years of my life. Most people would think that I am some hot shit, super awesome guy that everyone needs to know; I am just me. I don't think I am overly special. Yes, I am a lecturer in folklore and mythology across the country, an avid podcaster with over 900 followers and practice the alchemical arts of making potions, but I am just doing what I must do to survive. Booze and video games aren't free.

My childhood was descently normal, aside from the whole learning the mysteries of ancient potions and alchemical practices. I just didn't think anything of it, being able to affect the world around me with simple herbal mixes but it's just something I have always done. Thankfully, my mom found a tutor for that. It got kind of messy just playing around with the powers of nature by myself. Also, other odd things seemed to happen to me from time to time.

Take for instance, when I was a child alone in my room. I used to pretend that I was throwing a ball of air to the ceiling, like a beach ball. It would bounce noiselessly and I would toss it up again. All the while I was humming tunelessly. I was supposed to be doing homework, but thought this was a more worthwhile use of my time. I used the idea of an air ball because it didn't make any sound, unlike a real beach ball. Ma had started a load of laundry, which was right next to my room, and went about cleaning the rest of our modest house.

Here is where it gets weird. I absently tossed the pretend air ball too close to the light fixture on the ceiling and it nicked the glass light shade. You might remember what they looked like from back in the day. They were square, about fourteen inches across or so, had a screw base in the middle and were partly frosted over with some kind of swirly decorations on it. Yeah, the 'ball' hit one of the corners with enough force to shatter. I fucking panicked because there was no way it could have done that. It was all pretend, right?

I knew if I broke something else in the house, I would get in huge trouble. So, I did the most logical thing. I picked up a large chunk of broken glass and jammed it into my arm. I yelled from the pain but kept it there as the blood began to flow.

Now, the most fortuitous thing that happened was the washing machine went into the spin cycle. We had one of those old beasts that would "walk" if it was unbalanced, and it often was unbalanced. The bastard would slowly start to spin, then shimmy, then shake and before it was done, it would take huge steps to shift itself out of the cubby hole we had it in. We learned pretty quickly that we couldn't close the door because it tried to eat the door from the inside.

I learned much later we had a domovoy living in the base of the washer. You know, a little Russian house sprite that would help clean if you treated them nicely with offerings of bread, honey and milk, but would fuck your shit up if ignored. Yeah one of those bastards. We had no idea he was there, so he took it out on our poor washer during the spin cycle. The washer started going crazy, my air ball hit the fixture, glass started raining down around me and I stabbed myself with a shard. Hurt like hell, but in my panicked brain, it was a small price to pay to not get in trouble.

Mom heard the commotion, rushed into my room to check on me before dealing with the domovoy dominated machinery, saw the blood pouring out of my arm and freaked out. She rushed me to the bathroom to start tending to the wound, saw bone, practically passed out and demanded what I was doing! I stammered my partly rehearsed speech about doing homework, the washer went wonky and the light shade just shattered. I must have convinced her through sobs and tears. After a trip to the ER and a couple of stitches, we went and bought a new washing machine and mother fucking ice cream.

It was just my life. Odd things had always happened to me due to one unseen force or another. Such as, mythological creatures had always hung around me. Which is why I started studying them and not in a weird Hagrid or Newt way, I started studying the historical and folklore origins of the creatures.

Indiana University has a great folklore and mythology program, if you want to study the psychology behind them. I wanted to study the origins and documentation of the creatures. I used the resources at the library and forged my own secret degree. The one thing I cannot stress enough is to never deal with the fae. They are huge dicks. Now, that's not exactly their fault, the fae have a different more hedonistic approach to life. They do what makes them feel good, not what is defined as morally right or wrong by religion. To the fae, religion is an enigma; especially the Abrahamic faiths of Judaism, Islam, and all of Christianity, both Catholicism and Protestantism. That's a story for another day, though.

After college, My Friend Chuck™ and I went into business together selling Beanie Babies on Ebay, which failed almost as fast as we started. It was the end of the craze and no one wanted to buy with such an oversaturated market. He knows all about the mystical arts and what can be done, he just doesn't believe in magic. Anyone can do magic, you just need to believe that you can do it. Do you remember being a kid and believing in your whole heart that you could do something like moving an object with your mind or flying? Well, the mystical arts is just that; you believe you can do something and do it. I know it sounds too easy and that's the problem. People are jaded because of several factors like religion, television, social media, the list goes on. Due to the nature of the world of today, people believe what they are told. At least that is the belief of the practitioners of a small cult called The Believers in the Mystical Arts and Alchemical Sciences. I tried to subscribe to that theory and even had a mentor in college and shortly after, but only got through the beginning courses.

I studied the theory and practical things like potions and the basics of alchemy; but when it came to the manipulation of elements and transmutation, I failed every time. I had too much going on in my head all the time to clear it completely, as was required to move the forces of the world to my will.

"Yo Artie, you got any booze?" Declan looked at me hopefully. I knew better than to give a mixed race leprechaun booze, they turn into full blown assholes. Declan Callum Shaughnnesy-Golzales was a half breed fae; half Irish leprechaun and half Spanish duende, which are kind of like leprechauns, but without the shoe fetish. Only pure lines of fae have all of their powers. If they are mixed breeds, like Dec, their powers are diminished.

For those who are not in the know, leprechauns hail from the Emerald Island of Ireland. Known for wearing a tricorn, or three cornered, hat and fancy 17th century clothing complete with buckles on their shoes. Leprechauns were travelling cobblers and would make shoes for people with the gold to pay for their services. They usually didn't take much, just shaved off a bit to add to their pot. Typically, it was believed that their pots were stashed in completely inaccessible places, like midway up a sheer waterfall or at the end of a rainbow. That was complete hogwash. They kept the gold on them, just under their stylish hats. Typically, the cobblers were also tricksters that would do bits of nasty spells on the people that thought they could get away without paying or steal their gold. The spells ranged from twisting knots in hair to breaking pottery or spoiling food.

The duende are similar in their origins. However, they hail from the Iberian Peninsula. Known as the 'professor in the house', the duende were hostel dwellers that were helpful in more ways than just cobbling shoes. They didn't ask for much, just to keep the house tidy and in return they made sure evil spirits and vermin would stay far away. They also wore large three cornered hats and kept a stash of gold for their personal vices like tobacco and a stiff Spanish cheese.

Declan's mother was from Ireland and his father was from Spain, but they met in Santa Clause, Indiana. You know, the place that is Christmas 364 days of the year, but is closed for Christmas Day? They met, he wooed her with honey dripped rolling Rs and promises of eternal love. She batted her lush green eyes and softly lilted promises of house and home. Of fresh breads and the best shoes he'd wear in his life. It was a storybook romance that only Kris Kringle or Hallmark could write. Even though they had eighteen children and their youngest son turned out to be a pimp, they are still happily married and living in the city of love, Celebration, Florida.

Now, fae romances of the same species will produce pure blood lineages that keep the magic strong. Inter-fae species romances are more rare, but not discouraged however it muddles the blood magic and the outcome is uncertain whether the offspring will have powers from the father, the mother, both or neither. Declain was in the last grouping which is why he became a pimp to make ends meet.

It's even worse if a fae and a human have a baby. It is less about the innate magical abilities and more about the physical changes. Wings, horns, huge noses, pointed ears and even skin color changes are all side effects of that kind of pairing. Sometimes the effects aren't as noticeable, but then there are the oddities. These children are often shuffled around the foster care system for a while until they get lost in the system. You might be thinking, why haven't I seen a blue skinned person? Truth be told, you have. You're just not looking at them with the proper mindset. It's a rough life for them, but they do have sanctuaries now for the fae-touched or glamourlings.

I was about to answer him when my phone rang. Saved by the bell, literally. It was a call I was waiting for and dreading at the same time.

Chapter Two
November 1990

I didn't think about my mentor very much because he taught me and then just left. I have no idea if he is even still alive. I first met Felix Blau in my sophomore year of high school. He worked at the main library downtown Indianapolis. Living next to Garfield Park, there was a local branch of the Indianapolis Public Library, but it was really small and mostly catered to children.

The main branch, built in 1917, was a work of art by itself. It was originally designed by Paul Phillippe Cret who helped create many libraries, bridges and museums in the United States and France. Before the expansion finished in 2007, the main entrance was through the Saint Claire Street entrance. Up a flight of stairs, through the door and up a shorter flight of stairs you walked into the main reading room, which was just breathtaking. Two stories, almost completely lined with bookshelves with exits to the upper floor on the east and west of the room, it was an imposing sight with dark hardwood everywhere. The best part of the room wasn't at eye level, though.

If you craned your neck up, you were delighted to see a beautiful gilded fresco that had almost Egyptian altars and what appear to be Masonic symbols interspersed. There were three crystal chandeliers that had been refitted with electrical wiring to have bulbs instead of candles light the reading room. The floor of the reading room had computers to the right, the checkout counter to the left and books everywhere else. Small kiosks in the middle of the room had new releases, staff picks and books related to movies that were either going to be released or had just been released. Wide marble staircases were on the far left and far right walls that led to the tome studded balcony and further reading rooms.

The wall across from the entrance had the willcall window, a short hallway that housed offices and opened up to the slightly acidic scented stacks. My favorite place in the library.

Felix was one of the librarians that was in charge of the special collections. I had read through every bit of folklore and mythology found in the stacks and wanted more. It's not every day you get a fifteen year old asking for first print titles from Hans Christian Andersen or Joseph Campbell. Felix and I struck up a friendship mulling over "many a quaint and curious volumes of forgotten lore". He was the first to mention the Believers of the Mystical Arts and Alchemical Sciences. Well, technically I found an old passage in a Jewish rabbi's writings on Old English religious beliefs. Yeah, I was that nerdy even in high school. Felix was surprised I hadn't heard about the Believers before.

Before I ended my apprenticeship with him, he admitted that he placed that reading in my hands on purpose. The Believers are a very secretive group. If you don't know what to look for, it is nearly impossible to stumble upon the cult by itself. I'm sure some of you have alarms going off in your heads right now by me mentioning the word cult.

The term cult can be defined as a group of people that have sinister worship practices to deify Satan, but it simply is a way of defining the beliefs of a group of people that do not have a formal religion. The Catholic church did a lot of damage to ancient ritualistic practices, which were merely the beliefs of many ancient civilizations, such as the Greeks, Romans, Celts and even Jewish people.

The term religion didn't start until the Romans had changed from polythiestic pagans to Roman Catholics. *Religion* the root word of religion means reverence to God, as in YHWH, not Jupiter. Also, religion is a highly structured, centralized form of worshipping one deity with one main codex of rules and stories and a strong hierarchy of leaders. In especially the ancient Greece religion, each deity was worshipped slightly differently from state to state, city to city and even household to household. The practitioners would attach an epithet, or a description, to the chosen deity in which they would pray. It got kind of confusing.

Felix though, wasn't confusing. He was a tough, but tender old man. If you can imagine the picturesque elderly librarian, that would be Felix. Thick, horn-rimmed glasses perched on his nose, wrinkled, but with a full head of white hair. He smelled of pipe tobacco and Barbasol shaving cream and he always looked dapper in his crisp, white button up shirt, bow tie and suspenders holding up his slightly short pants.

Born in Frankfurt, Germany in 1927, his parents escaped to America before World War 2 broke out in Germany. They were some of the lucky ones. His father, Chiam, was a chemist by trade working for Ely Lily's son, Josiah K Lily. You know, the pharmaceutical moguls. They brought with them secrets that the Germans had locked up in their vaults about alchemical studies the family was conducting to transmute lead to gold and other impossibilities.

Felix never really spoke much about his parents, but the little bits I learned over the years were filled with laughter, love and tinged by sadness.

Chapter Three

Guilty As Charged

I hit the accept circle on my phone and before I could say anything I was assaulted with an aged female voice very loudly singing the Happy Birthday song. I sighed out loud, but was smiling. "Happy birthday dear, Arthur, my son, the love of my life, the joy of my jooooooys. Happy birthday to youuuu!" Yeah, she always knew how to both bring joy and pain at the same time.

"Ma, my birthday was yesterday," I grumbled and rolled my eyes in Declan's direction. He had heard her rendition of the sacred and cherished tune for several years now and giggled every time.

"Arthur Sydney Pax, do you really think I didn't know what day your birth was?" she started. "I, who bore you after twenty-two solid hours of labor without the help of modern medicine. I, who raised you by myself. I, who single handedly handled every boo boo, trip to the ER, heartache and sniffle. If anyone on this great green and blue Earth would know when your birthday is every year, it would be me. Besides, it's better to sing to you when you have a hangover." My mom, ladies and gentlemen, may not be Jewish by birth, but she is Jewish by guilt.

Diana Pax was a very strong and independent woman. She also kept a lot of friggin' secrets. The biggest secret was my paternal sire. Every time the subject was broached, she found a way to weasel out of the question. I think my favorite one was she "accidentally" sliced her hand clean to the bone during a routine phone call and required several stitches and several hours of time in the ER. Crafty old bitch. She raised me by herself and knew I was a special case from a very early age, being all inquisitive and shit. Mom didn't have a drop of magic in her, other than her magical way of annoying me and making me happy at the same time.

Would my life have been better with my paternal DNA giver? I don't think it would have been. Many fathers, not all, would try to teach their sons how to be manly and stop being such a child, blah, blah, blah. My mother was very kind and nurturing, but tough as nails when she needed to be. That kind of childhood was perfect for me and my budding abilities. Even though we didn't have a lot of money with only her income, I still had a fucking fantastic childhood.

"Thank you, Mommy. I love you too." That was the only proper response. Declan snorted and I glared at him. "Hey Ma, did you get the check? It looks like it hasn't cleared my bank yet?"

"Yes, Artie. I just haven't had time to go and cash it. Did you think I lost it or something?" She had a habit of misplacing things, but never money. I send her a check once a month to help supplement her meager Social Security benefits. The SS is good enough to pay for her bills and food for the month, but I like to give her a little "mad money" as she always called it. Whether she spends it or not is on her, but I want to make sure she is taken care of. I mean, she raised me and took care of me for half of my life, from birth through college, so I kind of owe her. "Oh, Artie, your Aunt Shirley called yesterday." Oh, boy, here we go. "She wanted to wish you a happy birthday, but for some reason she doesn't have your phone number. Did you wipe it from her phone again?"

Mom's sister, Shirley Grace was one of those staunch Catholics. Has seven kids, goes to St. John the Evangelist Catholic church, the oldest in Indianapolis, and is very against what I do. She usually sends me little digs about being saved and coming back to the flock, even though we were never Catholic to begin with. Holidays at the Grace house were full of tradition and Catholic guilt. We practically had high mass just to eat dinner every Christmas. Both she and mom went to Catholic school because their parents were also very devout believers, may they rest in peace. My grandparents passed away when the sisters were in their early teens. Even though Mom was made to go from a young age, she never fully accepted the lifestyle and Mom and Aunt Shirley went two different directions, religiously speaking.

Mom took their death hardest and turned her back on God, whereas Aunt Shirley almost became a nun. The only thing that stopped her from entering the convent was Uncle Roger. Captain Roger Grace was bold, dashing and a war hero just coming home from his tour in the Vietnam conflict where he saved an entire village of civilians from the evils of the Viet Cong. He then went on to convert the villagers to Catholicism. Even to this day, he gets mail from the citizens addressed to Saint Grace.

"I can neither confirm, nor deny that accusation, woman." I smiled from ear to ear. I had a friend that has a certain way when it comes to tapping cell phones and changing the internal memory.

"Dammit Arthur! You could at least try saying that without a smile." She was really pissed. She hardly ever swears directly at me. Sure, she has a healthy vocabulary full of colorful metaphors, but out of respect we don't swear at each other. "She might be a pain in the ass, but she's my sister and even though she has an odd way of showing it, she does love you. I've never seen her try to save someone as much as she does with you. I guess I am in the 'lost cause' category."

I sighed. "Alright, Mom. I will call her. I mean I guess I should set something up for Thanksgiving."

"Thank you."

"Yes, Mother." I hated the smug sound in her voice when she won an argument, but she's my Ma. She didn't say when to call her, though.

"Arthur, you should call her today." Damn, that woman!

"Yeah, yeah, yeah. Listen, I've gotta go, Ma. I need to call Chuck about a leprechaun and his pregnant wife. Some kind of disagreement on services paid." Declan winked at me.

"Arthur, I don't know where you come up with these crazy excuses to get me off the phone." If she only knew that my life is crazier than I can make up. "Anywho, I'll chat with you later. Love you!"

"Love you too, Ma." I always hated hanging up on her, but I've got things to do today. I made a quick call to Chuck to clear things up with Declan. He sent money through some kind of cash app, Declan saved the game, turned off the system and left with a snap of his fingers. Fucking leprechaun pimps. Peace and quiet reigned over my small domicile.

I really loved my house. It was built some time in the 1950s, kind of small with two bedrooms, a full bathroom in the middle of the house and a half bath in the master bedroom. There was a living area dominated by my gaming system and a small kitchen right behind it. In front of my bedroom was a den/study area that could be converted to another bedroom, but I needed that room for my books and work space. A sturdy wooden desk held my home office equipment; computer, printer, scanner, you know the usual. The spare bedroom had a futon tucked into one corner, but the rest of the walls were covered with bookshelves filled to the breaking point with books, scrolls, knick knacks and artifacts that I'd collected over the years.

There was plenty of room for a small family, but that wasn't on my docket at all. I know mom wants grandkids, but she understands that between my lecture circuit and my other full time job saving the world from the forces of evil, I just didn't have time for a lady love, let alone a family.

I went to the kitchen to grab a bite to eat before heading into my study to boot up the computer, start streaming some music, check my email and start working on my next research book describing ancient Jewish mythological monsters. Most people don't think about it, but angels and demons fall into that category. Technically.

The majority of my job is reading. Wading through the piles and piles of crap to find little bits of truth and draw the connections between this tale and that can be exhausting. Especially if it's in a different language. I know I previously mentioned that all you need to do when you use magic, is believe and it can be done, I wish that were true about understanding different languages. You see, practitioners of magic can affect the world around them. It doesn't work on the practitioner.

I have read about a wielder of the mystical arts that they can make someone believe that they have changed into a giant dragon, but all they are doing is affecting how others perceive the wielder. All of the senses of the subject, including their proprioception in regards to body size, are tricked into believing the image which the wielder is forcing to believe they see. Hence, the practitioner can make the subject see a dragon, feel the heat from the flames coming out of its mouth, smell the dry reptilian skin, hear roaring, taste the fear and feel as if they were standing close to an honest to goodness fire breathing dragon. The practitioner cannot physically change their body. Under the illusion, as solid as it is, the practitioner is still as they were.

I have tried to affect the words on the pages, scrolls, tablets or whatever I am reading to shift to English by using various potions, but to no avail. The letters would absolutely shift to Roman letters, but it would still be gibberish because my brain cannot translate the text; forget about hieroglyphics or pictographs, they just become positively pornographic. I had to either learn the language or call upon colleagues to help me translate, which was a good thing for me, because it gave me some fantastic contacts in the world of academia.

As I was reading through an email from one of my Jewish scholarly contacts, a new email popped up as The Proclaimers started their "da-da-dat-daas." I was going to ignore it, but the subject only said, "Liquid Dreams". I was intrigued, to say the least. I mean who knows what the meaning of the subject line is, it could be some tagline for a retailer, a new book, porn, a makeup company, you never know with these things. Clicking on it, I didn't see anything, other than the subject and the email address that sent it, www.liquidddreams.com. I was hoping for some kinky ass, busty lady porn, with the triple D's in the address, but alas. I disregarded it as spam and went about my day. Damn no weird email porn today.

I lost myself in reading and subconsciously humming to the tunes coming from my small sound system. I took notes the old-fashioned way, pen and paper. Chuck has always made fun of my stacks and stacks of notebooks I keep in one of my closets, indexed, appendexed, categorizedexed and with an ever growing concordance...(dexed). I don't trust this information on any electronic device, unless I'm writing a book or paper. My research notes have been with me since my freshman year at IU. God, those earlier notebooks are cringeworthy, but held some valuable insights and notes that I still use to this day. I will let anyone look through my little library as long as they do not eat or drink around them, nor leave them sitting out. I mean this is a little over twenty years of my life being poured into these books. I seldomly photocopied them and never, ever let them leave the house. Chuck borrowed one my sophomore year and it still has coffee rings on it and a poorly sketched pair of D-cups in the margins. Chuck was daydreaming about the lusty, busty librarian. I guess it adds character?

Before I knew it, my stomach was yelling at me like a twenty pound cat. "Shoosh you. I just fed you." I looked at my trembling tum-tum. Then, I looked out my window. Someone turned off the sun. The hairs on my neck started to prickle as if someone was watching me or I had forgotten to do something. I call it my Dumbass Sense. It's kind of like that arachnid kid's danger sense, but it only goes off for me when I am being a dumbass. I looked at the time, 9:30pm. Shit, I had forgotten to call Aunt Shirley. I set an alarm on my phone to call her in the morning. It was a trick I picked up over the years. Need to remember something important? Set an alarm with a message and a really annoying ringtone. I set it to "Baby Shark". I had thought about setting it to the Ballad of Gilligan's Island, but that just makes me think about Emily Dickenson poetry. You know you can use her poems and sing them to Gilligan's theme, right? Go ahead, look it up, I'll be here.

Chapter Four

Interlude: On Magic and Death

GOOD afternoon and thank you for coming. In this lecture series, I will help dispel common misconceptions of the fantastical world of mythology and folk tales. I am Arthur Pax and I am going to start this series with a look at a small ancient Mystery Cult from Medieval England. There is no official name, however research has shown that the practitioners simply call themselves the Believers in the Mystical Arts and Alchemical Sciences. A tome was uncovered in a hidden archive in Salisbury Cathedral in England, which is a short drive to the infamous druid historical site of Stonehenge.

This tome is believed to be from the early to mid 13th Century and handwritten in Old English. In the style of the Book of Kells, there are beautiful pages of Insular Art adorning throughout. This is the first and only surviving written evidence of this cult. It had been long spoken about in the scholarly world of Academia as an ancient urban myth, but with this new evidence, there is even a possibility that there might still be survivors of this cult in the world today. Other evidence found in the archive as well as writings from around the world give credence to this theory.

Today, I will be reading to you an excerpt of that tome, translated from Old English:

"In the season betwixt Autumn and Winter, there is a season of magic. Most people don't recognize this as a season, for to the casual person they flow seamlessly together. Believers know that not to be true.

"Magic is all around us. Druids believe magic comes from ribbons of power that connect together in certain confluences called lay lines. The Roman invaders believe that magic is a gift from their invisible sky deity named El or YHWH in which they worship. Believers know that not to be true.

"Also, magic isn't some illness that affects the world around us. It is not something that is passed from sire to progeny. It is something that even the common farmer can use. All it takes is Belief and the will to affect the world around them. Magic is something older and far more frightening than ever explained. Even for those of us who Believe, it is difficult to explain.

"We who Believe, follow a different path than most people. We believe in everything and nothing. We believe that magic is just a part of life, much to the detriment of those who are religious. Miracles, healing, protective invisible spirits such as angels - these are all part of magic, but they think this magic is from their God because they believe it. There is nothing inherently wrong believing in one supreme deity that controls all aspects of life, however that is only part of the picture. The grander scheme is much harder to explain. Moments of magic happen all the time, that most people don't see or know about.

"One such occurrence is the season between Autumn and Winter. There is no name for the season, but it can be sensed if you are properly attuned."

As we know, many scholars state that according to the Roman calendar, this season starts the morning of October 31, or All Hallowed Saints Day Evening. The Coligny Calendar, also known as the Continental Celtic Calendar, also states that the season starts with the ancient Irish celebration of Samhain. It is believed in many cultures now that this is a time of the year that the seen and unseen worlds are closest together. Spirits of the dead roam about the physical world. Most of them are still unseen or unfelt by the normal person; however the Believers, have a slightly different view.

Their primary function, according to the text, is to be gatekeepers between the world of the living and the afterlife. Most people and religions believe in an afterlife, even those who believe in reincarnation. While the idea of reincarnation has its benefits, it is based on how much money you had in life or how many good things you did. The afterlife also isn't a place that has a section for the good and a section for the wicked, like Heaven and Hell or Valhalla and Hel or Elysium and Hades (the Greek form of Hell). Nor is it a prize to be won by being wealthy or good like most people are taught.

They believe it is more like one giant mosh pit that everyone is put into for all eternity. The dead simply go about their lives in another plane of existence. Also, you can't get reserved seating in the kitchen. Someone does their job during your life. They do the mortal coil shuffle and start doing just as they did previously, in the afterlife as indicated in the text, and I quote:

> *"The afterlife is merely a different plane of existence. A life is ended and continued in a different realm of consciousness called the Phase Plane. The Phase Plane is all encompassing. Most spirits are content to continue life in the Phase Plane, however, there are some spirits that are restless and will try to return to the Mortal Plane.*
>
> *"Our primary duty is to not allow the crossing of these incontent spirits. We must also stand ever vigilant to stop the forces of evil from pulling spirits from the Phase Plane."*

It goes on to describe the optimum time for the spirits to try and cross over. Have you ever been out in the countryside as the season turns from Autumn to Winter? If you have, you'd notice steam rising from ponds, rivers, and lakes just before the sun rises. The scientific reasoning behind this is that the temperature of the groundwater is cooler than the heat of the rising sun. This effect is a form of evaporation. However, the Believers in the 13th Century did not have this explanation. They looked at it as spirits rising from the afterlife to cross over to the Mortal Plane. This fear was heightened after Samhain and before the first snows of the season, around the American Thanksgiving holiday. It is usually in dawn's light that the phenomenon is witnessed.

> *"For it is in the time in which Aurora is awakening, Shades are most restless. They long to roam the Mortal Plane as they did before. Some Shades are innocuous, howe'er some are violent and malevolent and only wish to continue to cause harm to the living and they will seek to do so by any means necessary. We are to stand ever vigilant and stand watch over the sites most frequented by Shades."*

The Shades cannot cross over at any time because, according to the writings, the two planes are out of sync with each other. This is due to a phenomenon that both planes are in opposite orbits around the sun.

Have you wondered why there is always someone looking at waterways? Lighthouse keepers, coast guards - hell, even swimming pool lifeguards - they all watch the water. According to the philosophy of the Believers, as long as someone is looking at the water, then all will be right. Especially if the water is used heavily by people.

While there are many ways for Shades to cross over, water is the easiest way for Shades to cross the Planes. Water is all three states of being at the same time: liquid, solid, and gas. Do you ever wonder why that whole Bloody Mary thing started? Water. The legend states that if someone were to say her name in the bathroom mirror at midnight the vengeful spirit of Mary Queen of Scotts would come and kill the person incanting the spell. Normally she won't bother to answer, but if you say the name with any amount of water in the sink, she will fuck your shit right up because she can cross over. Even if it's a few drops from brushing your teeth. Same thing with ghost legends and fog. A pirate coming to look for his treasure with his bloodthirsty crew will appear when the fog is at its thickest every several years. Fog is a form of water and makes it easy for them to slip over.

Are you scared of water, yet? Well, you should be. Think about all the creepy stories about water - Davy Jones, La Llorona, the Great Flood, the Bermuda Triangle. The list goes on and on. Well, it's all because water is the strongest bridge between both planes of existence: the Living Plane and the Phase Plane.

Does it get crowded in the Phase Plane? Sure it does, but since everyone believes in something different, it gets all sectioned off. Catholics, Muslims, and Jews are kind of lumped all together. Whatever you do, don't tell the Protestants! They think they are the only ones there and are positioned *just so* to attempt to maintain that illusion.

In summation, the Believers are adamant that good, bad, and indifferent Shades are all put together in the afterlife. There is no Heaven or Hell; there is just the Phase Plane. With the overcrowding and jealousy issues, some of those Shades try to jump out and back into a host body or try to cross over in certain watery places. That is the steam you sometimes see rising out of water after Halloween and part of their duties are to make sure that those Shades don't get out.

So, the next time you see someone standing in a field next to a small pond, they could very well be working to help save your life and keep the Shades where they belong. It's a thankless job with terrible benefits (i.e. none), but nonetheless an important one. Someday, I'll have to tell you about other things that go bump in the night, because they totally exist. For now? Stay clear of bodies of water that are steaming in the early part of the day. You never know what might try to latch onto you.

Chapter Five

Enter the Dame

I got up from my desk, stretched and went to use the facilities. I tend to forget to do things like that when I am in research mode. I heard the buzz of an incoming message on my phone, finished up what I was doing and went back to grab the phone. Fourteen messages and three missed calls from Chuck. I was worried he might be in trouble, so I scanned them. No, not in trouble, just being needy and a bit drunk. He was at Rackham's Respite and was demanding that I should join him. I just sent back, "Be there in 15." I ordered a car driving service and went to the bathroom to check out how I looked. Not terrible, I just needed to run a brush through my hair and beard. I tidied myself up, did the sniff test of my pits and went to find new clothes to put on. By the time I finished the driver was at my place and we were off.

It was lightly raining outside and just downright cold. If the temperature dropped a few more degrees, this rain would be snow. The first snow of the season was always a bane or a boon to everyone who lived in snowy areas. You know that meme that shows Will Ferrell as the overly excited elf and Sean Bean as the stoic, weary warrior? Yeah that's the reality of it. I'm in the middle; I hate that I love it so much. I was always sad when the spring rains came and washed away the last dregs of the frozen water particles. Granted, by that time, It was usually grey and covered with dirt and car emissions. It looked nothing like the white fluffy flakes that fell from the sky. It looks like the grumpy, old man who lives on your block that has seen some shit in his life instead of the fresh faced young woman with all of her life ahead of her. You know which ones I'm talking about. The driver delivered me to The Respite safely. I Cash Apped him some funds and a hefty tip. I mean he drives people for a living from one bar to the next. I'm sure he has seen some shit.

Looking at the outside, it looks just like any other neighborhood bar, where the working poor go to unwind after a long day of drudgery. On any given day from the moment they open "Promptly at 1pm," until last call, it is never empty. Sometimes, there is a line of day drinkers waiting for the owner, James Rackham, to open. The brick building had two windows flanking the door. Both were plastered with stickers, posters and community notices. This was every bit a local bar. If you grew up in the neighborhood, you knew where it was. It's the kind of place that if your mom or dad wasn't at home, they were there. There were no weekly specials, there were no high falutin drinks being poured. It was a simple place for simple folks completely covered in pirate memorabilia. The owner was a bit obsessed with real life pirates, not that "BS Hollywood shit," as he would say.

James was a bit of an oddity. He grew up in a small town in North Carolina, Greenville to be precise. If you don't know much about the Carolinas, you should know these important facts. They have swamps, mountains, coastlines and was home base to one of the most notorious pirates, Edward Teach, also known as Blackbeard. I'm sure you saw that pirate movie with Barbossa and Teach. His real life was much more crazy than anything Disney could make.

Teach and John "Calico Jack" Rackham were contemporaries of each other and were both pardoned in 1718 and 1719, respectivly, in New Providence, an island in the Bahamas. During the end of the "Golden Age of Piracy" many pirates were pardoned and given a new start in life. Teach moved to North Carolina after terrorizing Charles Towne, South Carolina. Rackham stayed in New Providence and met the love of his life, Anne Bonny. Sure, she was married at the time, but Calico Jack was a larger than life figure.

Shortly after Rackham and Bonny hooked up, he stole another British sloop and took off with his lady love in disguise as a male crew member and added, the also cross-dressing, Mary Read to the roster.

Now, neither women knew that they were of the same sex, their disguises were "so good." The only way Bonny saw through Read's disguise was when Read confessed her feelings to Bonny and Bonny in turn confessed she was a woman in disguise. Read returned the confession about the imposter clothing. In fact, Read said so many confessions to Bonny it was like a diocese close to Easter, and they started up. Calico Jack caught wind of his lady having an affair with another crew member, unbeknownst to him that his partner was in love with another woman and then the fun really began.

When the entire crew was finally caught on November 15, 1720, Calico Jack was tried and hung. The ladies, on the other hand, "plead the belly" because they were both impregnated by their captain. I think I watched that porn once, they called Poly Pirates: All Aboard! Mary Read died while in captivity of a fever and sadly so did the baby. Anne Bonny gave birth to a son and disappeared from history.

James Rackham knows the rest of her history. He is very secretive to other people, but he shared his family history with me. Anne fled with the child after he was old enough to set sail and they both landed on the Carolina shores. They lived off the land for a while, scraping together money from their trapping and skinning business and whatever they could steal from unsuspecting neighbors. They bought a small parcel of land and lived on it until Anne passed away in her sleep one spring evening. From there, it was marriages, births and deaths in the family line. His infamous great-whatever grandfather, was the key to his obsession. James had all of his family records put in a lock box, in a safe, under his bed in an undisclosed location in the Carolinas.

I opened the door and was greeted with glares and grumbles as the frigid wind whipped in before me. It was just after ten and most of the bar denizens were well on their way to a good rolling drunk. I quickly shut the door and they went back to contemplating their lives, one beer at a time. My Friend Chuck™ was at his usual booth. It was perfectly situated to see the entire bar, from the front door to the bathrooms and all of the regulars knew it was his booth.

Chuck had gotten himself a reputation in the neighborhood as being an upstanding guy. He was in the heating and air business and most of the people in the neighborhood only called on him, Silver's Air Service. His slogan was to "Give the Silver's Excellent Service, Guaranteed." I'm sure he "serviced" quite a few of his clients. I caught his eye and he frantically waved me over. I slid into the booth, opposite him and within seconds a beer magically appeared in front of me and I took my first chilled sip of the evening. I smiled at Suzie, the evening server and told her to go ahead and open a tab. She was cute, blond hair, mid twenties and a curvaceous body that shifted nicely as she worked. After taking a drink, Chuck exasperatedly sighed at me.

"I've been trying to get a hold of you for a while now." He rolled his eyes. "Were you sleeping, working or just jerking it?"

"Cool your jets, Turbo, I was busy working. I just lost track of time." I took another frosty sip. James knew the perfect temperature to keep his taps no matter what time of year it is. For American piss waters, it was a few degrees above too warm, for imports it was either right below ice cold or room temperature. Guiness is so much better at room temperature and chunky, like they sell in Ireland.

Chuck scanned the room with a small look of desperation. "Where the fuck is she?" he mumbled. Then the crowd parted and I followed his eyes to see a vision of beauty. She was tall, thin, pale blond with ice blue eyes and wearing something you'd see coming out of an opera house rather than at a shithole bar, in shades of pale blue. He pointed victoriously and exclaimed, "Eureka" under his breath, which means, "I have found it." While she was stunning, she wasn't my type. If I were younger, I'd be all over Suzie the barmaid, but alas, she was already dating someone else. Ah well. Chuck's eyes told me he intended to make her his latest notch, but I had a feeling it would go quite differently, if he approached her.

She was sipping a glass of red wine, which I honestly had no idea that James kept red wine in stock, personally I'm more of a beer and gin drinker, so I never bothered to find out. She had a look of curiosity mixed with boredom as she sat on her stool. Her back was so straight you could plumb lines from it. Her pert breasts peaked out of the cerulean colored dress, saying to the rest of the patrons "If you tried to touch me, I could decapitate you like a mantis." Her legs were crossed at the ankle and the boots she wore could make even the most conservative hooker on Washington Street blush. She was just Chuck's type.

I looked him straight in the eye and said, "Flat out no. No chance, no way, no how. Don't even think about it. Dude, she looks like she is a side piece for the Russian mafia and you don't need to be mixed up in that world again."

"Aww, come on Artie. She's been here for the past two hours, has had most of that bottle and keeps looking over here from time to time. I can see it in her eyes, she wants someone to go talk to her and I'm the classiest guy in this joint." He looked as if he was going to get up and stopped.

"What? Are you going to give her the 'Silver's Excellent Service Guarantee?' Come on Chuck, you don't even know…" I stopped as a hand was placed on my shoulder. I was so engrossed in dissuading Chuck from becoming a statistic, I hadn't noticed anyone approach him. I looked at the neatly manicured fingers placed on my right shoulder. They looked expensive. The arm attached to them somehow looked expensive as well. I followed the path up until I was staring into the icy void of her eyes. She was tall, thin, pale… you get the idea.

"Mr. Pax." Russian accent, of course it was Russian. I looked at My Friend Chuck™ and silently said, 'told you so'. "I wonder if I might borrow a moment of your time? It is to discuss a business matter." She gave me a slight half smile that sent shivers down my spine. It was a question, but the look said it was non-negotiable.

"Uh, yeah, yes." I hated it when I stammered. I am very fucking eloquent if you put me in front of people, but when it comes to one on one conversations, I am a blabbering idiot. I scooted towards the middle of the U-shaped booth and she looked at Chuck with an inquisitive gleam. "Oh, sorry, this is My Friend Chuck™. He's one of my business associates as well."

He rose slightly, extended his hand and said, "Charles Silver, at your service," with his cheesy as fuck, I want to eat you for an evening snack look. She very lightly touched his hand as she sat. He missed the part where she wiped it off on her dress as she put her hand down. Very smooth and subtle. I mean, he's not bad looking, black hair, blue eyes and a smile that could melt an igloo after selling ice to the Inuits inside. He had made many friends with that smile. Her face became unreadable as she looked from him to me.

"What kind of business are you looking for, Miss…" I fumbled for her name.

"My name isn't important, but the matter at hand is. My sister is missing." She stated curtly.

"Sorry lady, I'm not a private investigator. I am a researcher and lecturer," I countered. Her eyes went from blank to hard.

"There are those who would beg differently, those who Believe. Mr. Pax, I am not here to play games. My sister is missing and I need you to help me find her. If she is not found there will be terrible consequences." I heard the capital B in her statement and knew she needed my other services. I looked at Chuck and he knew when to leave in a conversation like this. He nodded and stood up to go chat up some of his regular customers with the patton-pending smile he shifted from person to person. I pulled out a notebook and pen to write down the details.

"My sisters and I have never been far apart from the day we were born. We would work, come home, or even go on dates every once in a while. When our sister, Allie went out for a bit, we were surprised. Out of all of us, she was the most homebound. She told us she met some guy on one of those phone app websites. We were very excited when she said she was going out, so we didn't think anything of it. That was three days ago." Her eyes turned glassy, filling up with unshed tears. "Mr. Pax, we would all be beside ourselves if anything happened to her. We need her. The world would be less if she were gone."

I asked her all the pertinent questions; the who, what, when, where, why and other's motives. No enemies that they know of. Not a normal job that's 9-5. Not much to go on. She invited me over to her place to look around to see if I can find anything. I set it up for the next day.

"Mr. Pax, the longer she is gone, the more perilous our situation becomes." She placed her hand on top of mine. The chill that was outside the bar was still on her hand. I know she had been in the bar long enough for the chill to be gone. Surprised, I looked at her eyes and momentarily lost my breath as the chill intensified to become almost painful. Her face was empty of all expressions as she met my eyes. With that, she stood, as lithe as an ocelot and left without another word. I took a moment to mentally review everything about her as I rubbed my hands together.

Chuck watched her leave and he quickly filled the vacancy she left behind. "So? How'd it go?" he said with a smile, expecting some kind of sordid detail because he saw her touching my hand.

"Client confidentiality, Chuck." That wasn't a very satisfying alliteration, but it'll do. The rest of the night, we drank and talked about our copious college conquests. That one was better.

Chapter Six

March 1996

"ARTHUR, you need to believe that you can do it. Search deep inside yourself. Remember a time when life was easier and you were younger. Search your memories. Search your feelings for those memories." Felix sat on a stool above me with his legs crossed, looking like a skinny, tiny Buddah.

"I am trying, Felix." I whined in reply. I really was trying to believe that I could move the ball in front of me.

"Do or Do not…" Grinned the Jewish Yoda. I sighed and concentrated harder on believing that I could move the ball in front of me with just my will. I had been at this for the better part of an hour and there was no movement. Just the sound of the blood pumping through my ears, the in and out of my breath and Felix's judgement.

I had been his apprentice for five years now and had come no closer to being able to use the Mystic Arts as he called them. I simply thought of it as using the Force. I mean, what teenager wouldn't want to use a mystical power that could literally do whatever you could imagine? I just wish that it worked for me.

I had no problem with the practical stuff like mixing potions and finding the proper ingredients. Some of the ingredients, believe it or not, can be found in the produce section of the grocery store. Rosemary and oregano are common enough ingredients that any variety will suffice, but things like mandrake root and some of the more dangerous poisonous plants are harder to buy. Sure, now you can just buy them on Amazon, but when I was a teenager, Amazon was in its infancy and still had a lot of kinks to work out. Ebay was a decent place to get some of the harder to buy stuff because it wasn't as heavily policed in the mid 90s, but you knew what key phrases to use.

I sat with my eyes closed until a timer went off. That wasn't the end of the lesson, but the signifier that a new potion was finished and I was super eager to give it a try. I looked up at Felix with a twinkle in my eye and he nodded. I jumped up, eager to get away from that damn unmoving ball. Some of the Believers said that for potions to truly work properly, you also needed to put some of your will into them. If you believe the potion to be more potent, it will be. I haven't found that to be true.

Sure, I put my heart and soul into making every potion I brewed, but I couldn't feel the ebb and flow of the Mystical Arts as I did so. I had a few massive failures when I was just starting out, but it was usually due to me rushing or adding the wrong amount of this or that. After one huge failure that nearly gassed me completely out of Felix's house, I learned to be more cautious and careful. Elderberry wine and mustard seeds really make a terrible smell when mixed with doe urine. It was supposed to be doe milk, the jars were right next to each other and I was in a hurry. I know they look completely different. I learned the hard way.

I know you're probably questioning what that combination makes. Felix uses it as a rheumatism relief balm. The elderberry and ground mustard both have high anti-inflammatory properties and deer milk is higher in casein protein than regular milk to help rebuild muscles while he sleeps. Sure he could use any other milk to fortify the concoction, but he says he prefers the flavor of deer milk. I just haven't figured out who milks them.

I got to the table, just as the candle under the potion went out. Felix had set it up this way as a failsafe way to boil his potions while he was busy. It was kind of brilliant because the tealight candles he used burned for only an hour at a steady temperature of one hundred and seventy degrees which was perfect for most of the potions he brewed regularly. Like this one.

Felix's notebooks say this potion was supposed to cause unbridled flatulence for twenty minutes. I was planning on using it on My Friend Chuck™ to get him back for a prank he pulled on me. Although, putting a fart brew into his beer was probably a bit over dramatic for him building a Solo cup fort around my bed while I was sleeping. Sure it was a mild annoyance, but this was our Junior year of college and we'd been pranking each other since day one.

I put on an oven mitt to take the three neck distilling flask off the stand that hung about a half inch from the tealight. I knew it needed to cool but I wanted to make sure there was no odor. Wafting the steam towards my nose, I didn't detect any sulfides from the brussel sprouts nor fermented duck egg yolk. Nor did I detect any of the high temperature yeast that would make it react to the beer and speed up the process. I only smelled the sugary sweet smell of the corn syrup that would help blend in with the Rolling Rock that he preferred to drink. I thought it tasted like corn with carbonation and didn't like it. My cheap beer of choice was good old fashioned Miller Genuine Draft. It didn't taste like American piss water, but got me plenty drunk. Also, back in the day, it was a great way to impress the ladies. If you had a bottle of "the champagne of beers" and a pipe in your other hand, the ladies thought you were more sophisticated than the normal Bud and clove cigarette crowd.

I poured the strange brew into a mason jar to let it cool and make it easier to transport. The pale beer color would hide perfectly in Chuck's Rock. Making it practically untraceable and the perfect prank. He would never know what hit him. I just hope he doesn't shit his pants. Gas is one thing, but unexplained poo is another level altogether. Not that it wouldn't be funny, I just didn't want to tarnish Chuck's reputation, just his pride a little.

I let the mixture cool a little before testing it out. Normally, I would test out my potions on myself, if they were harmless enough, but with this one, I didn't want to risk it. Felix was out of the question since he knew what the effects were. I had to find someone, or something that wouldn't expect it. Then, the answer came walking in the back door. The doggy door to be precise.

Felix owned two pets; a cat named Cat that I swear had its own pocket dimension it uses to disappear into and an old basset hound named Doodle Snufflelumpkins. It was Doodle's turn to check the effectiveness of the potion. I know people will argue that it was borderline animal abuse to do animal testing, but honestly, Felix does it all the time and this potion is very temporary.

I got an eye dropper and put a couple of drops in her water bowl. Doodle waddled up to it and lapped greedily as Cat watched from the couch in disdain. There was a glint of evil in Cat's eye as if he knew what was about to go down. Cats are creepy. It took only a few minutes before the first rumble rolled around Doodle's stomach. She looked up at me with suspicion and almost fear. Then, the first blast came rumbling out. She jumped, ran toward her bed with her favorite blanket and buried her head to hide from the onslaught of noxious fumes.

Because I only used a couple of drops the effects lasted about five minutes and the smell, oh, the smell. Words cannot describe the smell. I called the experiment a success and left to go give Chuck a taste, or rather a sniff of his own medicine.

Chapter Seven

November 16, 2014
Indianapolis, Indeed

THE next day came early, but not too early. I rolled out of bed and opened the blinds only to see the world covered in white. The first snow of the year had settled over Indianapolis, covering a multitude of trash and sins just in time for Turkey Day. I just hope the weather holds up. No one likes going to the Circle's "tree" lighting ceremony when it's slushy out.

The Soldier's and Sailor's Monument was once the tallest structure in downtown Indy, but over time, it stayed the same size as the buildings grew around it. Standing over 280 feet, it boasted fountains on the east and west sides and was the focal point for many celebrations. The construction began in the middle of what was called Circle Park in 1888 and was completed in 1901. It was dedicated to the soldiers from Indiana who fought in the Civil War. The center of Indianapolis was drafted by Alexander Ralsten, who incidentally was one of the architects of Washington D.C. If you pay attention to how Indy is laid out, you can see many similarities between the two cities.

The Circle of Lights festival started in 1962, as most Hoosires know. This winter festival is usually held the day after Thanksgiving and is one of the longest traditions still celebrated in Indy. Imagine, if you will, over 4500 lights strung up from the top of the monument to the surrounding rail. It's a big to do for us. Indy boasts they have the tallest "christmas tree." It's just made of stone and copper. The festival is a really big to-do every year. The mayor comes out and does his speeches, Indiana born celebrities, local churches and high school performing choirs come out and sing. The performances continue throughout the season. Those poor high school kids coming out in their show choir outfits and freezing in the snow just to entertain the tens of people who are willing to listen to them. At least they built a shelter that can house a large choir for the less than clear days.

Snow made everything more magical and special, I was hoping that it would still be wintery white for the next few weeks for this year's upcoming ceremony. I can only count on one hand how many times I have been able to attend, but it was always fun and was always snow covered. I also went with my mom the previously aforementioned times. Sure we didn't have a huge amount of money when I was a kid, but Mom always found a way to make life fun and going out in the snow was always fun for us.

There were many winters spent at Garfield Park, on the south side of town, sledding down "Suicide Hill." I had this plastic, circular, red sled, with yellow handles. That thing could fly down the hill. I know it's not very PC to call it "Suicide Hill," but you have to understand, the hill stopped at the road that winds through the park and back in the 80s and 90s, there were no safety rails. As far as I know no fatalities were ever claimed, but there's always those urban legends about "that kid I went to school with who died on the Hill." I know there are steeper and more dangerous hills in Indy, but this one was just my speed.

I know I've been rambling here for a bit, but you have to understand, this entire inner monologue happened in the span of time it took me to look outside, go to the bathroom and get coffee brewing. It's funny how remembering and thinking thoughts always are faster than you can verbally say what just happened in your brain. I have had full conversations with myself and it took five times longer to explain to My Friend Chuck™ what went on in my brain.

I knew I had a long day ahead of me, but I remembered I needed to call Aunt Shirley, but I needed coffee and a shower first, but I couldn't forget to call, but, but, but. Ugh. I just wanted to pretend for a few minutes that I had no responsibilities. I debated on taking a bath, but it's winter and it's cold. I decided on a shower, at least that way the amount of chill will be offset by the sauna I created in my small bathroom and there will be hot coffee when I was finished.

After a quick break of my fast and the cup of liquid adrenaline, I ordered a car service to drive me to my client's house. I realize I don't know much about the situation and what I am getting myself into, but I also don't necessarily get a bad feeling about taking this client. I have worked with other clients in the past, not as many as an infamous wizard in Chicago or a demon witch in Cincinnati, but I have helped out my fair share of people and Fae. Monsters, on the other hand, I've had quite a few run-ins with them.

Most people don't realize that they are around us all the time. Normal people see them, but dismiss the image of the creature as either something completely mundane or just part of the scenery. Centaurs in the wild become regular horses, hydras become swamp weeds. Only the people who are truly looking can see them for what they are and most people call them crackpots or conspiracy theorists.

I hear there is a group of people out west that actually research and help monstrous creatures. I'm sure most people who have dealt with them just consider them a kookie bunch of nerds. They sound alright to me.

A raven made a ruckus outside my window to draw me from my thoughts and he was right. It was time to go. The driver messaged he was at my house and I left. It was a fairly quick drive to the house of the sisters. The gated drive was a bit imposing, but they lived in Irvington and seclusion was part of the village's past. It was founded in 1870 as a suburb of Indianapolis, but by 1901 was incorporated into the rapidly growing city. Many private people, like generals and artists lived in the quiet rural area, originally. There are more old houses in Irvington than most of the rest of the city. It is one of the few historic districts preserved by some kind of high falutin' society. The gate wasn't overly imposing, like I have seen before, but it came with an official "historic" plaque and a private residence sign.

Rising above the driveway was a beautiful brick two story house with a fucking turret on it. Kind of made it look like a little castle. The driver nervously dropped me off at the door and sped away. Now, don't get me wrong, Irvington has come a long way from it's exclusionary and isolated origins. It's one of the few communities in Indy that has community festivals and gatherings. This house on the other hand just gives off don't fuck with me vibes. It was quite beautiful with the covering of untouched snow shrouding the house and surroundings. It looked like a funeral shroud, but nevertheless a shroud.

The grounds looked as if in the spring and summer boasted a beautiful, lush garden surrounded by the brick abode. A couple of evergreen trees stood guard by the gate and several skeletal trees, either oak or maple dotted the rest of the grounds. I spotted a black bird watching me from the branches of one of the naked trees. I couldn't tell if it was a crow or raven but somehow it fit with the decor. I was surprised that behind the house a large garage that resembled a barn stood, unused. There were no tire tracks in the snow. I assumed they did not have a car, but horses might not be out of the question. I chuckled at the thought of horses in Indianapolis. The only ones I have seen were for either the mounted police or the carriages that charge exorbitant amounts of money just to take lovers from the canal, around the circle and other sights worth seeing.

Thankfully, the steps were clear and ice free, I did a quick jog up and knocked on the door, while rubbing my hands together. I find wearing gloves to be bothersome, because you have to remember to take them off and put them back on. I have pockets, so I live on the wild side in the winter. Also, if my hands are covered, I lose that important bit of tactile sense. There was a small flurry of activity in the hallway behind the stained glass door. The activity was distorted by the bevelling of the glass and the myriad of colors on the door. There was no official picture, it was just abstract shapes, mirroring itself. Quite lovely, but not as lovely as the face that opened the door. She had vibrant red hair and a smile that lit up the entryway. Shorter than me, she looked at me with expectancy. "You must be Mr. Pax?" she asked hopefully in a soft Russian accent with a voice that was much deeper than I expected. It was melodious and slightly hoarse like a jazz singer.

"Yes I am. Arthur, please. And you are…"

"Oh, yes, sorry, my manners skip away when new people come to visit. I'm Danni." She ushered me in and closed the door behind. Offering to take my coat, she led me to a pale pink parlour with a cozy fireplace on the far wall. I gave her my coat, because it felt completely rude to not give it to her. She wore a dark red dress that looked antique, possibly even as old as the house, but it also looked new as if she had ordered it off Amazon just a few weeks ago. Danni also looked about the same, ancient but young, which was odd because she couldn't have been a day over 30. She flittered out of the room with my coat calling out, "Company!" Flittered was the perfect word to describe her movements, she moved with the grace and speed of a hummingbird. I heard the sharp staccato of heels on the hardwood floors and I turned to see the mystery woman from last night.

"Mr. Pax, I see you have arrived punctually. Thank you. I apologize for my anonymity from last night. I tend to be a very private person. You may call me Rochelle." She gestured to a sitting chair near the fireplace. Antiques seem to be the decor for this room, and most of them looked pre-Soviet Russia, which is very difficult to come by. I sat in an Imperial era armchair that had a small tea table next to me. Strong black tea and an equally strong pipe tobacco suited the feel of this room. Danni came back in with a tea tray, as if reading my mind. I tried to hide my surprise, but it must have been there because she just smiled at me mischievously.

The tea tray was beautifully worked silver polished to perfection. There were three cups and the silver teapot. I was confused by the lack of sugar, cream or even tea bags. She poured the dark looking brew into the delicate floral cups and passed them out, keeping one for herself. I politely took a sip and was pleasantly surprised by the flavour of summer berries, ginger, honey, cinnamon and a hint of spicy heat. It was delicious! *"Vasha zdorovye,"* Rochelle said ceremoniously before sipping her brew.

Danni repeated the toast and looked at my querulous eyes. "It means 'to your health', Arthur."

Rochelle gasped, "Sister! How dare you speak so informally to our guest. Have you learned no manners?"

I raised my hand, "I told her she can call me Arthur. So, no Fae rules of etiquette have been breached."

Rochelle smiled and laughed. "Fae, Mr. Pax? If that is what you think we are, I will allow it. To some cultures we could be considered part of the Fae. Yes, I guess that will do for now."

A long uncomfortable look jumped between the sisters and Danni looked chastised, as we all three sat quietly for a few moments sipping our beverages. I broke the silence to change the subject. "What kind of tea is this? It's delicious." Swirling it around in my cup I could see that it was a dark purple and not brown like regular tea or coffee. The spice slightly numbed my tongue and the warmth blossomed throughout my entire body. My senses and mental acuity seemed to be on overdrive with each little sip. I wanted to greedily gobble it down, but I didn't want to appear boorish. It seems that pororiety was more than just for looks in this house.

Rochelle smiled slightly, "This is no tea, Mr. Pax. This tisane is much older and more hearty. It is called *'sbiten'* in Russia and has been served much longer than tea from China. It is both a medicine and a comfort. Some provinces make it like *kvass* and are served slightly alcoholic. I prefer the more natural and sweet version."

Kvass is like drinking alcoholic rye bread. The main ingredient is rye bread that has been toasted until it is almost burnt, then fermented naturally. It's an acquired taste, but I enjoy it. Almost as much as I am enjoying the *sbiten*. Danni mentioned another Russian honey drink, much like mead, called *medovukha*. The main differences between the two are *sbiten* is always made fresh and if you want to make it alcoholic, you add wine instead of water and *medovukha* is brewed with hops. I'm not a huge fan of hops in American beers because it always makes the brew taste like a salty ballsack. And, no, don't ask how I know what a salty ball sack tastes like.

After some small talk about the weather and the upcoming holidays, we finished our *sbiten*, of which I was smitten. I even went as far as to ask for the recipe, which Danni gladly agreed to share. I took out my notebook and Rochelle knew it was time to get to business. She apologized and expressed the need to be quiet while looking around, because her other sister was sleeping, "she worked overnights." Danni went about cleaning up and busied herself with tidying up the already neat sitting room as Rochelle led me up the stairs. Mauve carpeting went up the curved staircase. Fucking mauve?

She led me to the front corner and opened the door, inside was a grey room that had the turret in the corner. It was a beautiful shade of grey that looked like a stormy sky. Rochelle excused herself to let me do my work. It was a typical bedroom, the queen size bed took up a good portion of the room. There was a dresser, and a vanity, but no closet because an ornate wardrobe took up the majority of a wall space. In the turret, there was a window and a small desk with a laptop on it. I checked under the bed and in the other furnishings for anything that looked out of place. I paid special attention to her lingerie drawer. Not because I was a pervert, but because it is usually a good hiding place for journals and the like.

My search turned up nothing out of the ordinary. I mean she had great taste for her special knickers, and looking at the size, she was fairly average size. I know that saying average size is subjective. My Friend Chuck™ thought that people like Rochelle were average size, but that was a bit too skinny for my taste. I love a woman with curves and well proportioned. Judging by her outfits, I could tell she would definitely make my head turn. Slightly goth in her taste but not too dark nor too scene. Scene is the term for what I used to call "dayglow goth" or goth with colors. She wasn't in the Steampunk crowd, because that's just brown goth. There were black shirts, gowns, skirts, hosiery, a couple of those pentacle shaped boob harnesses or whatever they are called. There were also other clothes in shades of purple, dark greens and one or two bright pink pieces. I looked around her bed one more time, feeling between the mattress and box springs, but came away with nothing. I did find some of her hair on her pillow. Long and a vibrant shade of purple that faded to a medium grey, I pocketed it. You never know when you could use someone's hair. It is useful for a myriad of spells and other magical workings.

I made my way into the corner turret, which was surprisingly roomy and despite the window was quite cozy. Between the house heater and the large window trapping the feeble light of the sun between the curtain and the velvet drapings that lined the walls, I had no problem with being cold. I opened the laptop and booted it up. There was no password protecting it. I guess she didn't have many secrets that she kept from her sisters. The background photo that came up after loading, was one of four young women. Two of whom I had seen just minutes ago, one with purple and grey hair, which must be Allie and the last looked like a twin of Danni, just with dark, straight hair. I took a photo of Allie to file for the case and yes, she was the type that would wind me up like an early 1900s pocket watch.

I was able to access her social media, email and other pertinent files and start scanning them to get a clue as to where she had gone. There were a lot of potential suitors, so it was going to be old fashioned detective work for me. Or just hack it by using magic. It was always an option, but not the one I wanted to over use. Sure, I would sneak on Aunt Shirley's phone to delete my number, but that was me being a dick. If I had her phone, it would be so much easier to find out who she went to meet. I jotted a list of the last 10 people she had both emailed and sent direct messages with and went to close the laptop. An email snagged my attention. The subject just said, "Liquid Dreams." Clicking on the email, it was the same as the one sent to me; only her email address and the weblink. I made a note to look at it when I returned home.

There was nothing else to see on the desk. In the drawer there was a little, yellow notepad, which I took out to inspect. The top page was torn off. I thought to myself that it couldn't be this easy. I found a wooden pencil and rubbed the paper lightly to see if anything was written down. A picture started to show so I sped up only to find a hastily drawn pair of boobs looking back at me. Sigh, goth and she doodles boobs? It's as if she were my soulmate. I heard a door open behind me and turned to see Danni coming from what looked like a bathroom wearing only a towel. I could tell by her wet hair she had just come from the shower, but for the life of me, I couldn't remember hearing any water running. I really have to stop focusing so hard when I am working. I looked her over and liked what I saw. She startled when she saw me on the computer.

"Oh, Mr. Pax, you have been so quiet I completely forgot you were still here." She looked mischievously confused as she winked at me. "I was only going to borrow a few bits of her clothes. We do it all the time." I remained silent. She took a few steps toward the wardrobe as my eyes watched her lithe body. She stopped and turned to me. "Are you going to just sit and watch me? Maybe I will give you something better to look at." Like an owl floating down to scoop up a field mouse, her towel fell soundlessly to the floor.

Huh, Danni was a natural redhead.

Chapter Eight

Interlude the Second:
A Discourse on Unkindness, Murders, Parliaments and Corvidae

THE avian corvidae family has roots all over the world, whether it is jay birds, rooks, jackdaws, crows or ravens. Some subspecies of corvidae can be found. The most common are crows, ravens and rooks. Their very distinct song, for lack of a better word, can be heard for miles in the quiet of the wilderness. It is a call that has sparked images for countless ages, as well as stories, poems and songs. Many of the Native American tribes of North and South America have some kind of tale about one or more of the corvid brothers.

Many of the Pacific Northwest tribes have a tale of how Raven turned from a strikingly beautiful white bird with the voice of a songbird to clad in all black and having a croaking, guttural song. The story has many variations, but they all have the same basic threads. Raven was beautiful and fell in love with the daughter of another bird; owl and eagle are the leading two. Raven went to go steal the daughter and was stopped several times but he would not be dissuaded. He then figured out how to trick the father to let him play with the sun, which the father figure kept in his hut and did not share with the rest of the world. The father figure allowed Raven to have the sun to play with or he didn't and Raven stole it, either way, Raven got too close to the sun and it completely burned his feathers and the smoke inhalation forever changed his voice. This was his punishment for trying to steal the daughter and he gave the sun to the rest of the world.

Most corvids in the Americas have been branded as tricksters that played light-hearted pranks on the other inhabitants of the world before man came into it. In Europe, they were ill fated omens and harbingers of death. The Teutonic tribes believed a pair of ravens sat on the throne of Odin, the Allfather, and went out every morning to bring him news from the nine realms on Yggdrasil, the world tree. Named Huginn and Muninn they were his Thought and Memory, respectively. In ancient Greece, they were not only the bird companion of Apollo, the sun and poetry god, but Aesop used them in his morality fables. In the lands of the Celts, ravens were associated with the war triple goddess The Morrigan. Even in far northeast Asia, the raven is a fertility and creator deity called Ktukh.

Physiologically, the differences between the corvidae subspecies is not easy to differentiate for the majority of the subspecies. Ravens and crows are separated by size and beak or foot coloration. Jackdaws and rooks are of a smaller stature and beak structure. Jays are the most colorful of the corvids, specifically the striking blue jay. With his taunting cry, it is no wonder he is considered a trickster in the Eastern American tribes.

Most of the Corvids have the ability of mimicry, much like a parrot. Some can make noises to imitate other animals, sound effects, car alarms and even human speech. It is joked about that a group of crows or ravens should be taught to say the word "run" then let loose in a park with running trails. That would certainly make those miles go quite quickly if it is heard from above on a dark night's jog.

Corvids are also able to use simple tools, like sticks or rocks to get food. There have been many experiments worked with wild and tame ravens and crows that involved getting bits of food out of simple contraptions by using simple tools to obtain those objectives, such as sticks, rocks and strings. It only took a few tries to figure out the contraptions.

On another topic, in the English language, there is a part of speech called nouns of assemblage or collective nouns. It is used as a way of classifying a group of people, things or animals. Everyone knows of a herd of cows, a bunch of bushes, a pack of cards or a flock of birds, however, some birds have been further classified and some other animals have unique collective names such as: a clowder of cats, a skate of rays, a ballet of swans. Corvidae also have unique nouns of assemblage. Crows are known as a murder, ravens are called an unkindness, rooks are called a parliment, jackdaws are called a train and jays are simpy called a band. The next time you see a flock of corvidae, please be sure to use the proper noun of assemblage. It could be the difference of a simple unkindness or a whole murder.

Chapter Nine

Pleasant Run Parkway

MY eyes took in every inch of her 5 foot frame; pale but not sickly, lightly freckled, curves that would make a french curve ruler envious. Her smile went all the way from her toes to her eyes. And those eyes, those mellow, seductive blue eyes. My mouth was slightly agape when she first walked into the room, but by now, it was full-on gaping. I quickly shut it and put on a passive face to not appear too eager. I was mesmerized as she started to soundlessly make her way to the turret. My body started to betray my facial expression as nature took over. A few more steps and she froze as we both heard the clacking of her sister's steps walking in the hallway downstairs and becoming muffled as she mounted the stairs. Danni jumped slightly by the impending discussion on impropriety. Her entire body moved with the jump and slight aftershocks rippled on the less firm bits that protruded from her slight frame. She turned quickly, grabbed her towel and flitted away to the bath and shut the door with a soft click just as Rochelle walked into the room.

"Do you need anything, Mr. Pax?" She spoke with the professionalism of a tenured secretary. I didn't exactly trust my voice, so I started shaking no and I took a gulp. "I believe I have a few good leads to start with. There have been many communications between Allie and several gentlemen via email and several social media sites. I jotted them down and will do some investigating." I stood, feeling that the swelling had subsided enough to walk without giving myself away. "Could I also have her phone number to try and track the GPS on it. I have a friend that can help with that and to put your mind at ease, it will be completely confidential and not the local law enforcement agencies."

That seemed to put her at ease. She walked to the desk and took the pad and pencil. Frowning, she looked at me with one eyebrow raised in a question.

"I only did the pencil rubbing to see if she had written anything down. Old spy technique." I quickly defended myself. She only let out a slight sigh, wrote the number on the paper and tore it off for me. Placing the notebook and pencil down, she turned to lead me out of the house.

"I have already called you a personal driver, Mr. Pax. I will cover the cost of your expenses from now until you find my sister. Discretion, expediency and efficiency are the key to my happiness and the rest of your pay." She opened the door and I shook her chilled hand.

"You have my word, um, I never got your last name?"

"Zvezdochka. It means "Little Star" in Russian." Her lips turned enigmatically up. "*Dobrey diem*, Mr. Pax."

I walked out to find a black Ford Edge waiting for me with a professional looking driver standing by the back door of the car. He was about the same height as me with dark hair under his chauffeur's hat and wearing a long wool coat that went to midthigh over his polished black shoes. He looked almost bored behind his dark sunglasses. I walked up to the driver with my hand outstretched to shake his. He firmly grasped mine and said in a crisp British accent, "Mr. Pax, you may call me any time to take you where you need for the duration of the investigation."

"And what do I call you?" He handed me a business card, White with black letters that said "Claud" and his phone number. "Claud, huh? Any last name to go with that?"

"No, sir." He opened the door and closed it after I sat comfortably, then joined me in the car and asked for a destination. It looked as if he had a slight limp to his gait, but I blamed it on the snowy ground. I had no idea where to go first, so I simply told him home. He put the car in drive and started slowly pulling out.

I looked back at the house and in the turret window, I caught a glimpse of Danni with her finger and thumb in the international hand symbol for 'call me'. I didn't have her phone number, so I did the international shoulder symbol for 'I don't have your number'. She pointed to her phone and a second later my phone buzzed. Unlocking it, there was a text message that I opened. It was just a picture of her lips, light pink lipstick and she had her lower lip trapped between her teeth. My pants jumped again. What the hell had I gotten myself into?

On the way home, it started to snow again. I went over my notes on the drive. Claud drove along Pleasant Run Parkway, which was a beautiful drive out of Irvington that followed the Pleasant Run Creek, which began at Ellenberger Park and ended at Garfield Park. It began its life in the 1920s as a scenic drive and had been worked on and transformed into a hiking and bicycling trail in the mid 90s. It was one of my favorite roads to drive on. It gently wound from the east side to the south side of town. I stopped looking at my notebook at a stop light as the snow started to fall faster. The wind picked up a bit. "Be careful, Claud. It gets a bit slippery on the Parkway," I cautioned.

"Yes, Mr. Pax. I have driven these roads before. I have an impeccable driving record." Well good for you, Mr. Smarty-Pants... "I do like to keep my pants smartly pressed, Mr. Pax. Thank you for noticing." Claud had an odd smile on his face. I began to wonder if I had said that out loud.

"Um, Claud, I didn't mean anything by it." I felt my face flush. I normally don't have my inner monologue come out. The light changed as a big gust of wind rocked the SUV. I kept my mouth shut, because the last thing a driver needs to worry about in the middle of a snow storm was a mouthy passenger. Every foot, it seemed the snow intensified. The wind was howling, the trees were straining under the sudden weight piled on them and the onslaught of the wind. Claud was driving with a quiet intensity, paying attention to the road and the conditions around us. The wind howled again. A startled look came across Claud's face. He yelled to hold on as he swerved and sped around a large branch falling from an elderly tree. His quick thinking had narrowly avoided us being buried under a large amount of fresh powder, ice and timber.

My heart lept a few paces ahead of the car and Claud white knuckled the steering wheel. "We are almost there, dammit. You've been following us for a while, ya bastard, and you pick now to attack?" He was muttering to himself. Another howl, sounding like it was literally right outside the car. I opened my mouth to ask him about what he had said and something from the side of the creek slammed into the car, picked it up, tossed it and we were airborne. As we started our first revolution, my head hit the window and the world went dark. I thought I heard laughing.

Chapter Ten

Short Interlude
Snow

I have heard that there are over fifty words in the Inuit language for the English word 'snow'. To them, snow was just another fact of life like breathing and eating. It also shouldn't surprise you that there are hundreds of ways to describe how snow moves, the intensity of it moving and how it looks after it has fallen.

In the Russian language, it is common to simply say, "*Sneg idyosh*" which translates to "snow is walking" which has a beautiful imagery. Russians living in Siberia have just as much snow as Alaskans do and at one point the eastern point of Siberia connected to the western point of the land now called Alaska via a bridge that sank beneath the ocean approximately seventy thousand years ago. The Inuit people have shared DNA markers with many East Asian cultures, including Russians. The beauty and eloquence of the Inuit and Siberian people have helped them survive many centuries of winters.

When it starts to snow in the United States, many Americans simply say, "Fuck."

Chapter Eleven

April 1990

"OUT of the four elements, which is the most important, Arthur?" When Felix led with a question like this, he usually had a specific answer in mind. Normally, I can guess what it could be and beat around the bush until I nail it on the head.

Today, I just wasn't awake enough. I had stayed up late working on a book report on Melville's *Moby Dick*. It wasn't that I didn't read it, I read the book before the semester started, but really hated writing analysis reports on popular books, partly because everyone would write the same thing and partly because I was more interested in reading things like Hesiod's *Theogony* or Heroditus' *History*. I know at the age of 14, I should be more interested in comics, video games or whatever the latest action movie was to discuss it in length with the rest of the guys in my homeroom class. I just really didn't care that much. I mean, the last great movie released was Batman, but not much else can compare with Tim Burton's masterpiece.

Last night though, I wrote a seven page essay on the importance of not letting addiction overshadow sensibility then I played Sonic the Hedgehog. Okay, fine. Maybe I liked doing things that normal teenagers did, as well as expanding my mental horizons.

I sat in silence breathing for a few moments after Felix asked the question in quiet contemplation. I mean, fire is the obvious answer because without fire, there is no warmth in the winter, no heat to cook food on to destroy bacteria, no sun in the sky nor magma in the center of our planet to keep it rotating. Earth was important for growing plants to feed not only people, but what people eat. Air was the very breath of life taken at the moment of childbirth. Water was what helped sustain our bodies from becoming lifeless husks like all other living things on the planet. Each affected the other like a giant game of rock, paper, and scissors. I took in another breath.

"Air is the most important. For without air, people, plants and animals would die." I was for certain I was right.

"Ah, but what about bacteria, are they not important and some do not need air to survive?" Felix opened a book nearby. "Methanogens are bacteria that can survive in a completely oxygen deprived environment. Their primary function is to exchange carbon dioxide to methane gas in the digestive system of many animals. They are most prevalent in the digestion process of bovine species, which is why cow flattus smells highly of methane gas."

"Seriously, you have a book about cow farts?" I shook my head.

"Oh, my young pupil, there is much that can be learned about cattle digestive systems." He flipped a few pages back in the book.

"Yeah I know, a cow has four stomachs that help it digest its food." I was getting irritated because I'm sure he was beating around the bush to irritate me.

"Not so. A cow has only one stomach. However it is separated into four chambers, the reumen, reticulum, omasum and abomasum. Each chamber has a different function that helps them properly digest and expel waste. It's a much better system than most other digestive systems found in nature. But this has nothing to do with my previous question. Which element is most important?" Felix closed his book and put it aside. I knew if I wanted to get a nap before dinner, I needed to answer his question quickly.

I sat and thought in earnest this time. If air wasn't it, it possibly wasn't earth because there are plants that can be grown completely on air and water. Fire was very destructive, the sun burns unprotected skin, magma and lava destroy everything in its path, even a simple candle scorches the moths that are drawn to it. That means there could only be one answer.

"Water. According to many origin myths, the Earth was covered in water until a primordial force pulled the soil from the depths. Christian, Maori, even many Native American tribes all attribute water to be the life source of life. Water is needed by all living plants and animals. Even inanimate things like rocks and sand need water to either break down or move around." I felt very confident with that answer.

"Correct. Water is changeable, it can go between three states of being, liquid, solid and gas. It is used in many religious and cultic practices as a purifier. It is associated with fertility and is even present at the birth of all living creatures. Seeds need water to change and sprout and plants continue to need water to grow, mature, produce more seeds and even in death water is needed to help break down the cell structures by introducing helpful bacteria. Water is the most important element because it is needed by everything on this planet." Felix turned around in his stool by the workbench and picked up a pitcher and an empty glass. He poured clean water into the glass, put the pitcher down and took a long drink.

"You and I are changed every day by water. We need it to help hydrate every system in our body. We use it to wash off dirt and harmful viruses and bacteria. We even use it to see. If there weren't fluids in our eyeballs nor tears to constantly wet the eye, we wouldn't be able to see anything. We'd be as blind as a cave fish." He placed the glass down. "Now, water can also be harmful. If we drink too much, or it gets into our lungs we could die. Water makes landslides, floods, erodes mountains and destroys crops if there is too much or too little.

"Water, according to the ancient alchemists, was a feminine force, because to ancient alchemists, they needed to put everything in boy, girl and everything in between. Why you ask, who knows." Felix rose from his stool to gather a few beakers, bottles of oddly colored liquids and jars of dried herbs. "I noticed you are a little ragged around the edges. I'm going to show you how to make a cocktail that will not only clear your head up from the sleepies, but also help you with a hangover, when you get old enough to get hangovers.' He winked at me and we went to work.

Chapter Twelve

The Laughing Devil You Know is Better Than The Devil You Don't Know

NORMALLY, when I wake up, it is usually in stages. Stage one: feeling. I become consciously aware of the blanket surrounding me and the pillow my head is nestled on. Stage two: sight. I see my eyelids shutting out the sun as it is trying to creep into the perfect darkness. Stage 3: hearing. I can hear the sounds of the outside world, traffic, birds, the rain, when it happens. Finally stage four: bladder. The need to relieve myself is strong first thing in the morning. I came in a jumble of these stages. First thing I noticed was ringing in my ears. The blanket was hugging me very tightly around my waist and my head felt pressurized as if I had been hanging over the edge of my bed for a while. Something dripped into my nose, which was odd, because I was lying down.

Then my memory flooded back. I was NOT lying in bed. I was in the backseat of the SUV that had just been flipped. I opened my eyes quickly to assess the situation only to shut them again. Everything was jumbled. I couldn't tell what was where and it was bright enough to send a sharp pain right to my temples. My heart was practically leaping into my ears. I started breathing slowly to not slip into a panic attack.

Slowly opening my eyes again, the scene started to make more sense. I was upside down in the back seat. The window was completely shattered and snow was creeping its way into the cab. Claud wasn't in the front seat and there was an eerie laughing sound coming from somewhere outside just beyond my line of vision. I tried to move my arms, but lightning bolts of pain shot through my right arm. Great, either dislocated or broken. It was slightly pinned between my body and the door. My left arm was a bit sore, but usable. I found the buckle for the seatbelt and disengaged it. The second I heard the click, I knew my mistake. I fell into a jumble on the hood of the upturned vehicle and my body blossomed into a giant nerveball of pain.

After the pain subsided, the giggling voice came back around. A blue hand tipped with razor sharp knives shot inside the SUV from the back. It grabbed me by my coat and dragged me across the broken glass by my left arm all the while laughing like the Joker from the 90s Batman cartoon. Mark Hamill is spectacular in that role. It's odd what I think of in the middle of danger. At least I wasn't thinking of Danni? Well, now I am.

I was pulled to my feet, thankfully my legs were sore but undamaged, and spun around to meet my assailant. It stood taller than me, was pale blue skinned, had long, black hair that covered its eyes and was absolutely rippling with muscles. I mean, its six pack of abdominal muscles had an eight pack on top. It stood there naked in the snow with its knife fingers, smiling a maniacal smile that only truly insane people can.

A blood curdling laugh split the silence and its lips rising in pitch and fervor. I scanned the area looking for Claud, but I saw him nowhere. Not even his tracks, but the snow was still rapidly coming down. If this were to keep up, we could be looking at at least three to four feet of snow by nightfall. The creature released me and I fell. I scooted away as rapidly as I could and took stock around me for weapons. The only thing I could see was the falling snow.

The world slowed down. I felt the wind currents flowing around my body. I had no weapons on me. The only thing I could think to do was try to pack a snowball and throw it at the creature. One handed it was a bit clunky, but I started gathering the flakes into a ball. I whistled a little tune because in the past I noticed that things happened for the better if I focused while I whistled. The creature's smile faltered at the manipulation it was witnessing. It was as if there was magic being used, but I already knew that I cannot manipulate the mystical arts. However I didn't have time to contemplate that right then.

Just before I threw the snowball with all my might, I heard a sharp pop and the creature's head snapped to the right. It stumbled a few steps to catch itself and turned to face where the sound had come from. Like a dark angel, Claud stood with a pistol pointed right at our assailant, the barrel smoking in the frigid temperature.

Another pop and flash of burning powder came from Claud and the bullet hit the creature right in the forehead. It fell backward into the piling drift banks with a great plume of snow flying up. I looked at Claud and he positively looked bad ass. The wind whipping around his open coat, with a plain black suit underneath; white shirt and blue tie completed his ensemble. He looked more like an old west gunslinger in a modern corporate world.

"Are you alright, sir?" He started to quickly walk toward the blue man thing. We both had no problem seeing it was male since it was unclothed and had a rather impressive set of gonads.

"My right arm isn't exactly working and my bell was rung pretty damn good, but I'm good. What the hell is that thing?" I walked closer to the immobile laughing deviant. We reached it about the same time and the first thing we noticed was the snow was still white. We exchanged a look as both knife tipped hands slashed out at us as the creature once again jumped to its feet.

"Hee, hee, heeeeeeee. Your metal sling cannot hurt me, Mahaha!" its grin grew wider than possible. It was odd for the creature to throw in a villian laugh at the end, when previously all it had been doing was laughing and giggling. It reached out again as I packed another ball of snow and immediately launched it as fast and as powerful as I could muster in a few seconds. The creature flipped ass over teakettle in the air back towards the mostly frozen creek. Claud and I both looked in disbelief that I had knocked it out with just a snowball and we ran after the creature.

"Great, a mahaha, I thought I'd never have to face one again." Claud didn't seem to be running out of breath as fast as I was. Granted, he was in much better shape than myself. I kept up, though, as the adrenaline pumped through my blood into my muscles, extending them further and faster than normal.

"Why are you laughing like a criminal mastermind like in the comics?" Man I was out of shape, but running in the snow was damn difficult. It is not as bad as running in water, but you have to add the factor that you're running in frozen water.

Claud audibly sighed. "I'm not laughing at it. It's called a mahaha. Inuit trickster. This one is a particularly nasty one. I've had no problems dropping them before with a head shot." That revelation shook some cobwebs from my head. I probably have a concussion, but no time for that now.

I paused long enough to try and access my memories from a trickster course I had taken once. Right before I could remember, the Mahaha, jumped out of the tree line again, laughing its head off. I slid to a defensive posture as Claud fired off another couple of rounds toward the trickster. Claud's shots went high while I attacked with another snowball and the bastard just danced around everything we shot at it, all the while laughing and swiping at us with his talons.

I rolled out of the way of his claws towards the creek and a memory hit me. I jumped up and ran towards the water and scanned to see if it was completely frozen over or still running. I was lucky, there was still a lot of motion in the waters. Fuck this was going to be cold. "Hey Claud! Are you thirsty? I sure am thirsty from all this running around." and splashed into the stream.

"Have you lost your bloody mind?" Claud yelled between the shots. "This is hardly time to be drinking from that disgusting stream." The Mahaha whipped its head around to see me acting like I was taking a drink from the frosted waters. Sensing easy prey, it gleefully jumped towards me. I took another faux sip, one handed.

"Boy howdy this water sure is refreshing after all this working out. Are you sure you don't want any Claud?" I started to slosh my way out of the water downstream from the action. Keeping one eye on the Mahaha, I made sure to wade to a more shallow exit point. The bitter cold stream was starting to wear on me tremendously. The Mahaha looked at the running water and became almost transfixed to the spot. It was still eyeing everything cautiously. "You look thirsty, friend," it looked at me. "Would you care to take a drink?"

"I only thirst for your blood." That Cheshire cat smile almost had me jump out of my skin, but I held firm.

I tried another tactic. "If it's the iron content you want, this stream has plenty and unlike my blood, it won't get sticky and mess up your long locks." The Mahaha bent over eyeing me wearily. It reached a hand in to test the waters, literally. A lick of his tongue on one of his knife fingers verified my claim of the rusted iron content of the polluted stream. People had been throwing all kinds of metal in it lately, like old bikes, shopping carts, I even remember seeing a car bumper in it further upstream at one point. The iron content of the water was certainly fortified enough to resemble blood.

Tasting the delicious iron, the Mahaha crouched on its haunches and started to scoop up the water greedily, relishing the iron tinted ice water. I motioned to Claud to push the creature in. He motioned that he didn't understand and started to aim his gun at the base of its skull. I waved my arms frantically and again did the pushing motion. With a shrug, Claud rushed the beast and pushed it in. With a startled howl, the Mahaha fell face first into the stream and transformed into snow, which was dissolved and swept downstream rapidly. At that exact moment, the storm let up and shortly after that the sky cleared up completely. Claud and I were panting, cold and wet from the snow but sweaty from the heated activity and grateful to be alive.

"What the hell is wrong with you?" Claud started, "I had a bead on the base of its skull. Nothing can dodge that, unless it has eyes in the back of its head!" He reached his hand out to help me up from the water. I wish I had a heater in my clothes because even though the wind had all but stopped, I was freezing and would be dealing with hypothermia if I didn't get inside really damn fast. Claud reached into his coat and pulled out a flask.

"Drink a mouthful of this. It'll help heat you up." He unscrewed the lid and took a mouthful. I swear I saw steam coming out of the flask, but it must have been a trick of the weather. He handed it to me and without a second thought I put it to my lips.

Whatever was in the flask, tasted sweet like mead but strong like 151 proof rum. It was also really thick and coated my insides as it slipped down my tongue, into my eager stomach. Then, the damndest thing happened. I felt like my blood was on fire. It was more of the dying heated embers of a long slow burning hardwood like oak and not like the heat of a christmas tree quickly blazing until it is reduced to ashes. It also looked like my skin was steaming, but once again, I could have been seeing things.

"Thanks. That's delicious." I handed the flask back to Claud. "What is it, if I may ask?"

He capped the flask. "It's a mixture of my own, Olympic ambrosia and phoenix tears, keeps the chill away." He smiled a roguish smile.

"Alright, keep your secrets." Claud chuckled and shrugged his shoulders as I continued my explanation. "Anyway, you said that was *A* Mahaha, but I had a theory that it was *The* Mahaha, as in the father of his species. Normally, bullets will stop a lesser demon like them, but the elder Mahaha can only be gotten rid of by making it thirsty. I used a bit of subterfuge to put the idea in its head that it was extremely thirsty. After it stops to take a drink, all you have to do is push it in and it dissolves until it can reform up north where it comes from. That'll take a while because this creek flows south and ends up in the White River, which eventually ends up in the Mississippi. Knowing the difference between "a" and "the" is the difference between bullets or having a flayed skin as it slowly eats you."

We both took a moment to calm down before going back to the car. It was a total mess. Both of the driver side tires were blown. In fact, the entire driver's side looked like it had been wrapped around a tree. There were several cuts in the metal from the claws of the Mahaha. Most of the windows were completely blown out. Anyone looking at it would say there couldn't be any survivors. Obviously, they were wrong. Claud pulled out his cell phone and quickly made a call to have us picked up. We did the nervous shuffling as we waited. I thought about doing some small talk, but he was busy texting or something on his phone. He put his phone away and turned his attention toward me.

"You said the right arm, yeah?" I nodded and he started feeling around the shoulder. "Ah, it's just out of socket. On the count of three. One…" He pushed it back in place with the ease of an emergency room surgeon. I screamed with the ease of an emergency room patient.

"Dammit, I thought you said, 'the count of three!'" I yelled.

"Yeah, but you'd be expecting it and would clench up, which would make this much more painful." Claud had a point, but dammit, he needs to work on his bedside manner.

It didn't take long to be picked up, nor to get back to my house. Claud jumped out of the front passenger seat and opened my door. After I got out, Claud didn't get back in. He simply shut the door and started up the walk to my door. "Um, don't you have to go fill out an incident report with the owner of the driver service?" I inquired.

"Already done." He replied. "Besides, Mr. Pax. I have to wait for a new car to be delivered and I have need of your facilities."

"Ok. I'll start some coffee to warm up." I walked up and unlocked the door.

"I'd prefer tea and some gin." Of fucking course he would. I guess this gives me time to find a sling for my arm, do a little research and find out more about this mysterious sharpshooting, field doctor masquerading as a British driver.

Claud was less than forthcoming with personal information, but I did get out of him that he was ex-British Military and had been working as a personal driver for the past five years for the Zvezdochka sisters. He availed himself to my meager tea supplies, with a disappointed look on his face. After messaging a few more people he finally unbuttoned his suit coat and took a seat in the kitchen, all the while still wearing his sunglasses. Even though my right arm still smarted, it was much better than before. I took a handful of pain pills and opened my laptop to start searching the list of suspects.

My phone vibrated. I usually keep it on vibrate while I am working so the sounds don't disturb my train of thought. One buzz was usually a message, either email, text or social media message of some kind, two buzzes were one of my social media notifications, three buzzes was always my mother. It was only one buzz this time. I was kind of glad it wasn't mom, because I'd have to hear from her about not calling Aunt Shirley and inform her about being in an accident. If I didn't talk to her, I didn't have to tell her. I reached out and found another text from Danni asking if I wanted to have dinner later. If I said I wasn't tempted, I'd be lying. I promised myself I'd answer her later.

I sent out a couple of emails to some of my contacts, splitting up the list of suspects. It was faster to have several people working on the same list than having one person do it. These people I trust with my life. Confidentiality was key when it came to my secret keepers. With that done, I went to my living room and stretched out on the couch. Another buzz on my phone with Danni again. I hope she didn't end up being a stalker. I unlocked the phone and the message said "I have more information for you about Allie that I couldn't say in the house. Let's meet later." Buzz, an address and time. How could I say no to her? After about a half hour had passed, Claud finally rose from his kitchen chair and walked around the house. It didn't bother me too much because I was really tired. At some point I dozed off.

It was just light enough in the field that I could see the vapors of my breath coming out. The pre-morning light lit up a small pond as the leaves that had just fallen off the nearby trees surrounded the pond in the breeze. I looked around as the light grew. There was not much here, it was a bleak landscape. Everything stopped moving, the wind, the clouds, the ripples in the water. A fine mist started rising out of the pond. I couldn't move as from that mist a hand rose out of the water near the shoreline. It felt around grasping for something to hold onto. Grabbing a root that came out of the ground, the dessicated body pulled itself up enough to look around.

The fleshless head swivelled so the empty eye sockets could take in the surroundings. It threw its head back and let out a bone shattering howl. The pond looked like it was starting to boil. With each bubble that freed itself from the almost placid waters small howls answered the corpse. Fingers, arms, heads and other various body parts started rising from the depths. The mist over the waters started pouring over the banks as did the dead rising from the Phase Plane.

I tried to move and was stuck fast. My heart was pounding because I could only stand there in horror and watch as corpses rose and started moving toward me. My heart wasn't the only thing that was working. I tried to think of anything I could possibly do to get out of this situation or at least wake up.

Their howls filled the air. A veritable cacophonous cornucopia of chords clashed together and threatened to shatter my eardrums.

From somewhere behind me, a blinding red light shot out. The army of the dead stopped their wailing and turned together to face the source of light. The light reflected in the eyes of the dead that still had them. It was as if the light of the sun had been amplified and started burning away the flesh of the corpses. The wails turned to pure terrified screams of pain. All of the bodies out of the water caught fire and started burning rapidly. The smell was atrocious. It filled my nostrils faster than their wails filled my ears. I still couldn't move as they broke ranks and started running in every direction trying to flee the death ray, but miraculously none of the bodies touched me. One fell right in front of me, writhing in pain and with its last spasm, exploded. Bits of fiery flesh, bone and organs fell all around me. As the flaming skull came straight for me, I woke up.

flesh, bone and organs fell all around me. As the flaming skull came straight for me, I woke up.

Chapter Thirteen

November 17
Revelations and Such

IT was dark, but then that doesn't mean much in the middle of November. I checked my phone, it was just after three in the morning and I had emails, texts and a phone call that I had missed. I waited for my heart to slow down before sitting up. Apparently, while I slept Claud had left. I sat up slowly, feeling all the aches and pains that I incurred during the day but it was nothing I couldn't handle. The light from my phone screen helped me move around my house, not that I needed it. I have stumbled in this house for the majority of my life up until now and not much has changed. I needed some water, I stumbled to the kitchen and flipped on the light and jumped, shouting an obscenity. Claud was sitting in the dark at the same spot as before.

I wasn't sure if he was awake or asleep, he was still wearing his sunglasses. His hands were resting on the table and it looked like he was sleeping. I called out to him. No reaction. I walked over and waved my hand in front of his face, he grabbed it with a smile on his face. "I am quite awake, Mr. Pax. I only require a few hours of sleep a night."

"W-what the hell are you still doing here, Claud?" I stammered. "I thought you left a while ago."

"Oh, sorry Mr. Pax, I wasn't clear earlier. I am to be with you for the course of the investigation. My duties include but are not limited to, driving, bodyguard, medic and general arsehole." He removed his sunglasses for the first time. I was shocked to see the milky white pupils of a blind person looking back at me. The fuck?

"What the fuck, Claud? Where the hell are your pupils?" I jumped back. My dream came back to the forefront of my memory. It was as if I was looking at one of the corpses that had risen out of the innocent looking pond.

"Mr. Pax. I apologize that the appearance of my eyes startled you, but you need to have full transparency about my condition." He replaced his sunglasses. "Before you start asking questions, yes, I am blind. No, that does not affect my driving or seeing. Yes, I can tell how many fingers you are holding up. Yes, I am tired of that joke. No, you cannot tell me a blind person joke that I have not heard before. I lost the use of my eyes during my time with the British Army. My troupe was caught in the middle of a firefight in some waterless hole in the desert. A flash grenade went off right next to my head and the world went forever dark. It wasn't until I was discharged and my sight was fully given up on, that I gained my vision back. I am not sure exactly what happened, but one day, I could see again. Just not through my eyes. That is all I know about my situation and all I want to know. Did I touch on everything?"

"Huh." Was all I could say at first, processing this bit of information. "The fuck?" Was my next utterance. Then, "Huh." I was completely out of questions, which was a first for me. I walked over to the cabinet and grabbed myself a glass, then to the freezer and took out my bottle of gin that I keep in there for special occasions and sat down in a chair across from Claud mulling it all over in my head, the attack, the dream, the revelation. Huh. I opened the bottle and started drinking, forgetting about the glass.

Claud and I practically finished the bottle of gin. I directed him to the spare bedroom for when he fell asleep and crashed into the loving arms of my pillow top queen size bed. This time, sleep was generous and didn't give me any more fucked up dreams. Later that morning, I woke with the sun peering into my eyelids. I moved my right arm and it didn't hurt. Neither did the rest of my body, nor my head, which was odd. I rose to go through my morning routine of relief, coffee and something to break the fast. Claud was already up in the kitchen rummaging around. I could have gotten upset at his lack of privacy he was showing me, but he did save my ass yesterday.

I decided on taking a shower instead of my normal routine and after I was finished I smelled the coffee and some kind of cooked meat. I wandered into the kitchen after dressing and Claud was finishing up cooking what looked like a full English fry up. For those of you not in the know, a traditional English breakfast is huge. It usually consists of fried eggs, sausages, rashers (a thick cut bacon that isn't all perfect and straight like American bacon is served), tomatoes, mushrooms, fried bread and baked beans. He poured himself a proper cup of tea and started plating the feast.

"I took the liberty of doing a bit of shopping, Mr. Pax. Your pantry was a bit sparse." He looked very comfortable in the kitchen wearing his standard suit. The jacket was draped over one of the chairs and his shirt sleeves were rolled halfway up his manly, muscled forearms. He had a plain, white apron around his trim waist to guard his pants from any splashes. Not that he needed it, his outfit was still quite impeccably clean. "I always start my mornings with a fry up and a cuppa. A man in your shape could use the metabolism boost. I have already completed my morning workout. If you care to join me, you are welcome to, I start every morning sharply at 6."

I poured myself a cup of coffee and he handed me a plate. We sat and tucked in wordlessly. My mouth went into overdrive with the simple, but elegant flavours combining together. After we both scraped our plates clean, he stood up and collected the dishes and started working on cleaning up.

"Thank you, Claud. That was exactly what I needed."

"My pleasure, Mr. Pax. Now, I believe you have unattended business to do." With that dismissal, he turned away and set to work. How the fuck did I inherit an Alfred?

Back to my study to boot up my laptop and get my phone. First thing's first, I needed to call Aunt Shirley. She picked up on the first ring and bid me a happy birthday, even if it was belated. I wanted to make this as brief as possible, so I cut right to the chase telling her I will be at her house for Thanksgiving. No, I will be alone. Yes, I can bring some dinner rolls, as if she never makes enough and then I made some excuse about needing to answer the door. With that I turned on my music and checked my phone text messages. Most of them were from my contacts informing me that nothing was out of the ordinary with the list of people I gave them. Damn. Emails were pretty run of the mill. I messaged Danni back saying I would join her later this evening and went about my day looking up my list of names. I also needed to go to my "secret lab" to work on some potions. I didn't want to be caught as unprepared as I was yesterday.

Chapter Fourteen

The Lab

THE thing I love about my house, other than the fact that I grew up here, was the secret entrance to the basement. In the front library, there is a door that looks like a closet for all intents and purposes and on casual inspection, it was a closet. There was a bar for hanging clothes and a shelf that spans the length of the five foot space. It held some of my more special outfits, like my tuxedo, my IU graduation robes, my Jedi robes and my official Hogwarts robes. Ravenclaw, if there was any doubt. I know I am a giant nerd, but I really don't care.

The back of the closet was a cleverly disguised door that led down a flight of stairs to a neat, furnished basement, complete with cobwebs. I used to hate going down there when I was a kid because spiders really creeped me out, but I grew out of it when I started seeing how beneficial spiders can be for insect control and potions. I also hated that the entrance to the basement was through my closet when I was growing up. Before I redid the entrance to the basement, the door led straight down to the depths of chilled spider hell. I found ways to block the door. That didn't quite work for mom when she needed to go down there for something.

After Mom moved out to get a smaller place in a retirement community, I decided to conquer my fears of the basement and make the house my own space. It was a comfortable size for a basement, almost the entirety of the floor plan for the house. There was a storm cellar entrance in the back of the house that was covered on the outside with bushes and debris. A couple of windows along the south, west and east sides to provide daylight were also hidden in the bushes that lined the outside of the cute little yellow house.

Aside from the water heater, furnace, and a double sink, the rest of the space was lined with shelves of various herbs, powders, body parts of long forgotten creatures, and liquids. Everything was obviously meticulously labelled and catalogued in handwritten journals I kept on a bookshelf near the entrance. The interior had two large tables with anything and everything you can find in a high school chemistry lab. Burners, beakers, tubes, stoppers, mortar and pestles, you think of it I probably had it. Under where the kitchen was, a large fire pit sat directly under my stove and the flue rose up and joined with the stove exhaust to not attract any outward attention. I wasn't ready to share this part of my life with the common visitor to my house.

I immersed myself in reading and concocting some potions to help combat the cold. I hadn't read the books for winter potions in a few years and found one that called for Olympic ambrosia and Phoenix tears. That son of a bitch wasn't lying to me. It made me wonder what other secrets Claud was hiding from me but that could wait for another day. I lost myself in gathering ingredients, crushing, mixing, boiling, reducing and other general cooking things.

The waiting was the worst part, so I leaned back for a few minutes. I thought about the first time I set up the lab and brewed my first potion in this space. I had already finished my first book and was getting ready for my first book tour. My publisher John Knottlemann had set up a tour of several Indianapolis bookstores, which was a good mix of both independent and chain stores. I knew the first stop would be the biggest of the chains, Books and Nobulls. They had a strict no cattle policy posted on the doors of all 314 locations across the country. In the past they have rented out small theater spaces to house big authors. According to my sales, I was considered a big author.

My first title was an adaptation of one of my college papers that I felt needed expanding on. *How to Train Your Trickster* sold over a million copies in the first year. Knottlemann went from a small time publisher to an overnight success because of my title and honestly all I did was write about trickster deities and compare them to pop culture references. I must have hit the right nerve in the geek community and people were eating it up.

My new found fame was mind blowing and quite panic inducing, so my first potion I created in my newly finished workspace was one that Felix taught me for calm and clarity. I used it mostly during finals, which were always stressful for me. I know at one point he told me the official name of the concoction, but I always called it Felix's Fixer-upper. It wasn't exactly the most difficult, nor the longest potion I had in my arsenal, but it did take time.

After chopping, mixing, crushing and starting to boil the ingredients in my sparkly new beakers, I decided to close my eyes for a bit. I promptly forgot to set an alarm and woke to the horrific smell of burning rosemary, ginkgo and passionflower. It was very pungent, but no actual fires had been set that day. I roused myself out of my napping chair and cleaned up the mess to repeat the process. I was awake for the whole time this round and it took over a week to get the smell out of the house.

For the record, the event went without a hitch. I was funny, charming and just damn good at pleasing the crowd. As I was ruminating on the past, the shadow of Claud intruded in my space. "Mr. Pax, if you are to join Miss Danni tonight, you should probably start getting ready now."

"How did you know about that? I never said anything to you?" I started feeling like my privacy was on the line. Having him shop and cook was one thing, but reading my phone messages and coming into the basement? That was too far and I told him as much. He held up his phone showing me a message from Danni that explicitly detailed what she would do to him if he did not deliver me to dinner tonight.

Grinning from ear to ear I rose. "Well, I guess I have no choice but to go and enjoy her company. I will get ready."

"Very well, Mr. Pax. I have taken the liberty of placing a suitable outfit on your bed."

"Thank you, Alfred, that will be all." I finished up and went up to my bedroom. The cleaning could wait for another day. Claud chuckled at that, thank God. I found a nice outfit on the bed; a simple plaid dress shirt in blues and teal and dark slacks. Changing and running a brush through my hair and beard, I went to grab my coat. Claud was already standing by the door and out we went. It was warmer than yesterday and looked like some of the snow had melted, but my walkway was clean and ice free.

Chapter Fifteen

July 1994

"MAKE this lead turn to gold? Are you out of your mind, Felix? Everyone knows that is just hokum," I knew it was just a tactic to teach me a lesson, but this one was purely fantasy.

"Oh, you know everything about alchemy, then, yes?" Felix had a mixture of mirth and sternness in his expression. "What is the first writing about alchemy, then, Mr. Smartypants?"

"Which translation?" I knew I had him in a corner because I had remembered almost every translation of the Emerald Tablet of Hermes.

"Bacon's translation of *Secretum Secretorum.*" Felix leaned back in his recliner in his basement, as he often did when I was about to recite any of the myriad of texts he had me memorize. It wasn't difficult, since I had an eidetic memory. I just needed to think about the page that I read it on and boom, there were the words. My classmates hated when I did it.

"Trouth hath hym so, and it is no doubt, that the lover is to the heigher, and the heigher to the lower aunsweren. The worcher forsoth of all myracles is the one and sool God, of and fro Whom Cometh all meruelous operacions.

"So all thynges were created of o soole substance, and of o soole disposicion, the fader wherof is the sone, and the moone moder, that brought hym forth by blast or aier in the wombe, the erthe taken fro it, to whom is seid the increat fader, tresour of myracles, and yever of vertues.

"Of fire is made erthe. Depart the erthe fro the fire, for the sotiller is worthier than the more grosse, and the thynne thynge than the thik. This most be do wisely and discretly. It ascendith fro the erth into the heven, and falleth fro heven to the erthe, and therof sleith the higher and the lower vertue. And yf it lordship in the lower and in the heigher, and thow shalt lordship aboue and beneth, which forsoth is the light of lightes, and therfor fro the wolle fle all derknesse.

"The higher vertue ouer-cometh all, for sothe all thynne thyng doth in dense thynges. After the disposicion of the more world rynneth this worchyng.

"And for this prophetisyng of the trynyte of God Hermogenes it called Triplex, trebil in philosophie, as Aristotle seith." I knew I sounded pretentious saying it in Middle English, but that's how they wrote.

"And what does that mean to you?" Felix placed his elbows on the arms of his recliner and steepled his fingers in front of his nose. His eyes filled with a twinkle of delight as I recited the ancient text fucking flawlessly.

"In the simplest terms, everything is interconnected," I answered smugly.

Felix leaned forward, "If everything is interconnected, then that means lead and gold are interconnected, yes?" I nodded my head. "If everything is interconnected, then it could be possible to change the nature of one thing and make it something else, yes?"

"But not changing lead into gold," I countered. "If it were possible, then there would be a surplus of gold and a scarcity of lead. You cannot take something that is one thing and completely change its nature." I felt pretty good about this argument.

Felix made a noncommittal noise. "Okay, let's go to the kitchen." He rose and went straight to the steps without hesitation. I rose from my stool and followed him. The door to the basement opened up into the kitchen area, which was a bit narrow for my liking, but such was the style of the house. He had his two seat table in the kitchen for himself and whenever he had company over. There was a formal dining room, but he never used it. The carved maple table and matching chairs sat under a sheet to protect them from dust and cat prints. Although it didn't matter to Cat much because he liked sitting on the acrylic covered particle board table in the kitchen.

I scratched Cat behind his ears as I walked past him to wait for Felix to continue. His kitchen was a simple layout, the sink had a window over it that looked into the backyard, the fridge-freezer combo was to my left as I exited the basement, the stove was next to the fridge on the right, a corner cupboard held most of Felix's baking supplies on a lazy susan, which was a huge thing in the 1960s and 1970s. More cupboards lined the area next to the stove, around the corner until it met with the sink. On the right hand side was an island, which he kept free of clutter for his prep and baking needs with more cupboards facing the stove.

He really didn't decorate the kitchen with knick knacks and bric-a-brac, but it was a cheerful spring green with yellow trim. Most of the pots and pans were either copper or cast iron. On the island was a sturdy butcher's block and a meat grinder. An ancient Kitchenaid stand mixer was on close to the sink because there was an electrical plug over there. He had placed groceries on the counter.

"What do you see?" He pointed to the island with the groceries.

"Um, flour, sugar, eggs, milk, butter, salt and some vanilla. I am guessing you want me to bake something?" I didn't mind baking, I was actually pretty good at it.

"Very astute. I want you to make me a cake." He handed me a weathered index card from his equally weathered index card box with a simple vanilla cake recipe written on it. I took the card and went about finding the measuring cups, spoons, cake pan and other instruments I would need to make a cake.

"As you are making it, I want you to tell me about the ingredients," Felix smiled.

"Okaaay? Um, first I need flour." I reached for the measuring cup and Felix cleared his throat.

"And where does flour come from?" he simply asked.

"The grocery store?" I guessed.

"Feh. This is not time for your standup routine, Jerry Seinfeld. Come on, think about it." Felix's eyes started to smoulder and I knew it wasn't time for comedy.

"Flour comes from a plant, wheat to be precise."

"And it just grows out of the ground a white powder? Give me more."

"Of course not, it is ground up in mills."

Felix opened a drawer and pulled out a sheaf of wheat. Perfectly golden yellow and spiky. He rolled it around in his fingers for a few seconds as he looked at it carefully. "Why not just use this, if it's the same thing?"

I shrugged my shoulders, "You can't use raw wheat, it wouldn't look or taste the same as other cakes."

"But this wheat sheaf and that flour are the same thing, so you could say they are interconnected, yes?" He held out the wheat for me to look at.

I took it from his hand and rolled it like he did, examining the fat bulbs of grain, the spiked ends and how the stem seemed hollow. "Yes they are interconnected, but the flour has been changed to be easier to use. In the processed form it is more valuable for people."

Felix nodded his head. "And how was it changed?"

"I told you it was ground up in a mill."

"What does that mean, 'ground up in a mill'? Do they just throw this (pointing to the sheaf) in and mash it up? If it were that easy, wouldn't it be better to just buy the wheat instead of the flour?" I had a feeling this was going to be a trap of some kind.

"Well, no, I mean there is a whole process of separating the outer coating from the seed and grinding up the seed and making sure it doesn't have bugs or rocks or anything like that. Then, white flour gets a special treatment to make it change colors, but some is left to age naturally. It's not a very easy process." I really am thankful for watching

Mr. Rogers, Sesame Street and other children's shows that explained how things were made.

"Ah, so, you would say that the wheat in its raw form, isn't as precious as flour? It certainly is prettier to look at, it smells good, but isn't as useful without change, yes?" Felix took the wheat back and put it in the drawer. He crossed his arms. "If you can take that imperfect piece of wheat and change it by stripping it down to its bare essentials, then using a device, possibly made of rock or metal or something like that, you transform it to something more precious, yes?" I nodded and pondered the implications.

"If all things are interconnected, then that means that gold and lead are interconnected as much as wheat and flour are interconnected, yes?" I felt the noose tightening as Felix took a step towards me.

"I mean, yes flour and wheat are interconnected because one is the product of the other, but gold and lead are two different metals," I said triumphantly.

"Ah, but if you take a few layers away and apply pressure, wheat can be changed to flour. The same principle can be applied to gold and lead. Gold has three less protons than lead and by applying modern physics, you can release those three protons in lead, thereby changing the structure to gold. It has been demonstrated several times in the past." Felix pointed at the ingredients. "Look at the things I have put on the counter. Each of them has its own properties and can be eaten individually. Some just might not taste in the raw form than others." He looked at the eggs and vanilla. I had to agree with him there.

"If you combine these raw materials in the proper steps, not skipping, nor skimping, you will create something new that has the same outcome every time and is delicious, in my opinion." Felix pointed at the index card. "Now, make me a cake and think about using each ingredient and where they came from. These are part of a whole and if any of them are missing, or not used correctly, then the outcome will be different. This is why people do not make lead into gold."

"Wait, what?" I scratched my head. He lost me on that one. "You lost me."

"Heh. I'm sorry I got ahead of myself." Felix shook his head. "The Believers had the proper recipe written down at one point and it was debated fiercely for many decades. Some wanted to use the knowledge to create more gold for the believers to become more powerful and others didn't want to draw that much attention to their society. It was finally decided that the formula should be split and hidden. Many of the holders of the secret died and their portion was lost forever, but there is at least one portion of the recipe that has been preserved and is still in the care of a current Believer."

I started measuring out the ingredients step by step following them as I was contemplating the origins of each little bit I added to the stand mixer. "Are you the holder of that secret, Felix?" I paused and looked at my friend.

Felix burst out laughing, "If you think I knew even a part of turning lead into gold, that I would be living here, you have another thought coming." I joined him in his laughter. "Besides, for me to even consider making myself rich, I'd have to have a Philosopher's Stone and no one has made one of those since the Industrial Revolution."

I went back to the card. "It says I have to separate the eggs, put the yolks in with the dry ingredients, but whip the whites separately. Why not just mix it all together and dump it in the pan to bake? Isn't it all going to the same place?"

Felix sighed and shook his head. "What are the four elements of alchemy?"

"Earth, air, fire and water," I recited.

"Good, how do you affect an alchemical change?" He prodded.

"By combining the elements in a precise manner to bring the desired outcome." It was really tedious repeating this over and over again, but I knew if I didn't he'd find some menial chore for me to do until I toned down my sass.

"Exactly! That's exactly it, my boy!" Felix clapped his hands together as if I had unraveled the secrets of the universe. "Baking a cake IS alchemy. You have each of the four elements represented in the process of baking a cake. Flour, sugar, vanilla are all plants from the earth, milk is water based, by separating and fluffing the egg whites, you are adding air AND you bake it in the oven for fire. Don't you see, my boy? You are taking something less valuable and transforming it into something more valuable. You are basically taking lead and making it gold. Sweet, delicious, fluffy gold."

I shook my head at the analogy and finished his thoughts, "And if all things are interconnected, the same process of taking lead and applying all four elements, you can make it into gold." Felix laughed again and clapped his hands. I took a bow and turned back to making the cake. I might not get paid to learn this stuff, but some of the fringe benefits are worth it.

About an hour after the lesson was complete, we both sat down to a couple slices of plain vanilla cake and cups of ice cold milk in silence. Felix says that eating your reward should be done with quiet contemplation of a lesson well learned. I still didn't believe that he didn't have the recipe for transmutation, but I let it go for now. I mean, who wouldn't want to know how to make unlimited wealth?

Chapter Sixteen

A Date with Destiny

The vehicle that stood before me was the exact model of the one from yesterday, but grey in color. Claud of course beat me to the door of the car as I was locking up my house and stood with it open for me to slide in. The streets were mostly clear of snow already, which was surprising for Indianapolis. Sudden storms like that always take us by surprise and sometimes I am snowed in for a few days.

Traffic was light for a Thursday at the end of rush hour, which was more than likely due to the snow. I was half expecting to arrive at some fine dining establishment by Keystone at the Crossing, but Claud didn't get on any of the highways. He steadily drove towards downtown. I sent a text to mom letting her know the dreaded call to Aunt Shirley had happened. She sent back "Kk and :)". I love that my mom tries to stay up to date with texting trends and social media. Last I knew, she had a Snapchat account for her cat. She calls it her "kitty porn" but doesn't understand why so many sports team mascots follow her account. I still haven't had the heart to tell her about Furries, yet. "We are here, sir." Claud pulled the car over in front of a familiar restaurant, The Pasta Place.

As a child I loved two things on my birthday, cake and spaghetti. My mom had made a yearly tradition of us having cake for breakfast and The Pasta Place for dinner. Sure it is a chain restaurant, having at least one in every major city across the country, but for some reason, it always felt more like a local owned restaurant. Depending on which location you go to, it could look like the inside of a European tavern or a four star bistro, no matter how it looked, they all offered simple, rustic food and quiet alcoves for people to converse in peace. It was kind of odd that she picked The Pasta Place for our date because it was more of a family style restaurant. I expected something more upscale and classy, but nothing should surprise me about Danni.

Claud jumped out and quickly opened the door for me to exit the vehicle. As I walked up to the familiar doors, I saw Danni talking to the hostess. Looks like I was right on time. I took a moment to admire her through the acid etched doors that I had been through many times in my life. She moved with the grace of a swan and talked to the hostess with a smile that looked slightly flirtatious. Some more words were exchanged and Danni picked up a pen, wrote something down and coyly handed her the folded paper. At this point I could be upset and turn back to the car because she was hitting on someone right before our date. The alpha male in me could get all riled up and barge in there demanding what the hell was going on. However, the only thought was, "She's into women too? That's hot." So, I opened the door and walked in.

Danni turned and gave me her full attention as we met eyes. I flushed. She looked positively stunning. She was naturally beautiful yesterday morning when I met her. Today, she applied just a touch of makeup to accentuate her natural beauty. Makeup is just the paint that an artist applies to a canvas. Some people look at blank canvases, but not me. I look at a canvas and see the craftsmanship that went into creating it. From harvesting the raw materials, to putting it all together, canvases are already a work of art. Then an artist buys one and takes the years of learning and honing their skills to add to the natural beauty of the canvas. Danni had one great canvas and knew how to use her artist's palette to enhance that canvas.

I stepped up to her and she greeted me with open arms and a soft kiss on the lips. "Hello," she purred in my ear as we embraced. The hostess let us know our table was ready and quickly showed us to one of the more private booths. It was mostly empty in the restaurant tonight, but that wasn't surprising. Indy people like to stay indoors after a big snow storm and even though the roads were mostly clear, it was still cold outside. Apart from the birthday party in the main section, there was a scattering of a few couples and a handful of other patrons. The hostess placed our menus on the table, which was totally unnecessary for me, I already knew what I wanted, looking at Danni. Wait, woah… Did I really just write that? It's like reading a bad softcore porn story from the 90s. Danni and I watched the hostess leave with the same look in our eyes. "So, I guess you don't mind looking at other women?" I asked boldly.

"Hell no." She snapped her head back at me. "I don't mind it at all. I miss being around women that aren't my sisters." She licked her lips hungrily. I was hoping it was because of the thought of food. "By the way, I'm bi." It was a very casual admission, like saying she liked Coke over Pepsi. Not that it bothered me. I was about to reply when the server came up with a couple glasses of water, a loaf of their famous bread and a smile. Drinks and orders were placed. Danni also already knew what she was hungry for, which was a double order of spaghetti with meat sauce and meatballs. I ordered the same, because that was my usual order. The server left us looking at each other.

"So…" I started.

"So?" She laughed. I smiled at my nervousness. It had been a while since my last date and I had never been asked first. "Don't worry, Tiger, I won't attack you in public. You seem a bit nervous. Has it been a while since your last date?"

At that I finally loosened up a bit. "Yeah. I was just thinking that. I know this isn't just a social call. You mentioned you had information about your sister?"

"All in good time. First, tell me about yourself, Arthur." Danni was certainly good at the cat and mouse game. I was terrible at it and dating. Look at my track record: several one night stands in college and then, the ex-wife. Tonight, I was sitting across from a beautiful, vibrant, confident woman and I was intimidated. I also realized I hadn't said anything for a while. God I hope I didn't look like an idiot.

"Uh, not too much to tell. I spend most of my days sitting in front of a computer researching, checking emails and writing. A couple of times a month, I get paid to go give a speech at some university or lecture hall all over the country. My life is kind of boring." I fiddled with my water glass and took a sip. Not the best tasting, but it'll do.

"There has to be more to the story or my sister wouldn't have hired you. She only trusts certain people of a certain persuasion. So, you must be rather certain." She seemed to know exactly about my other job, or she wouldn't be poking fun at me. Her laugh confirmed that she knew.

"Well, I rarely talk about my other line of work with my dates. Not that there have been many. I've been too wrapped up in my research gig, I forget to even ask women out." As I took another sip, our food was delivered and Danni ordered one of their speciality drinks, a blood orange Moscow mule. I thought it over and that sounded delightful, so I asked for one as well. We both tucked in and enjoyed our first bites of the steaming pasta. "Care for some bread?" She nodded. "Shall I cut it in slices or just in half?"

"I usually just eat the whole loaf so you might as well go ahead and cut it in half, I can pack it away and I'm not afraid to get messy." I think I am falling in love with this woman. I cut the loaf in two and we continued eating until the server came back with our drinks. Taking a sip, I was taken aback. What a flavor explosion! She seemed to enjoy it as well. Her eyes closed as she took a longer drink, she audibly moaned and smiled.

"This is literally one of the best drinks in the state." She beamed at me before going for another forkful. "What? You look like you want to say something." I mean, of course I wanted to say something, but I don't want to look desperate. So, I went for charming.

"I never knew anyone who could look so good with pasta sauce on her mouth." I cringed that I had actually said that outloud. "Ahhhh. I mean, um, er…. Fuck. How do you like your pasta?"

She laughed at me with a full throat belly laugh. "Aww, aren't you cute when you're nervous. Don't worry, I won't bite you." She paused. "Yet." I must have turned five shades of red because she laughed at me again and took a drink. I sat and poked at my meal and finally cleared my throat.

"As delightful as all this is, you said you have information for me? I'm not trying to end the evening, nor am I trying to wrap up the investigation quickly. If your family is no longer a client, I would feel more comfortable dating you and believe me, I would love to get to know you better. It's a professional thing, you understand, right?" I looked hopefully at the ravishing Danni. Her face turned introspectively.

"Yeah, that does make sense." She sighed, I could see the mask of 'everything is fine' finally drop. I saw the pain and worry in her eyes.

"It's just been a long time since things were normal around the house. Sonja, our other sister has been in a very bad depressive state, Rochelle has been overly protective of all of us, then with Allie missing, I thought an evening out might help at least my state of mind, but to be truthful, I am scared shitless that she is missing. I mean, it could have been any of us. Why Allie?" A tear escaped the confines of her lashes.

I reached my hand across the table offering it to her. She timidly accepted the warmth and bit of comfort that touch can give. Looking up at me, she smiled slightly. "Thank you, Arthur." Then pulled back and grabbed her napkin to dab her eyes. "Look at me. I'm a mess. I'm sorry to unload on you like that."

"It's okay. I am here to help." I hoped it came across as gently and gallantly as I meant it.

Our meals forgotten, Danni looked back at me very seriously and took a deep breath. "I don't think Allie went on a date. I am fairly certain she went out to check out a new club in town called Liquid Dreams."

That bit of information hit me like a ton of bricks. The emails I had been ignoring came back in a flash. I opened my email on my phone and found the link. I clicked on it and all that loaded was a picture with the club name in purple neon over a door. I tapped on the door and it opened. A scroll floated out of the door and unfurled. "Congratulations on being in an exclusive list of attendees for the opening of the new experience, Liquid Dreams. This is more than just a club, it is everything you have ever wanted and more." Then it had a date and address. I showed it to Danni.

"That is exactly what Allie received. She showed me and was very excited. She made up the whole date thing to get out of the house.

The reason I wanted to tell you this away from the house is because Rochelle is very controlling, especially in the winter. We all have our jobs to do and winter is when she is doing her job, so she is in control of the house." She paused to see if I understood what she was getting at.

"Kind of like Seelie and Unseelie fae?" I inquired. Most people associate the Seelie court with good and the Unseelie court with bad when it comes to the fae, or faeries as they are more commonly known. But it was more Summer for seelie and Winter for unseelie. Full blooded fae don't exactly have the same morals as humans. Their actions are dictated by the season. The summertime was when the Seelie fae were more powerful and the same for winter and Unseele.

"Similar, but more directly related to the weather and snow versus rain. Rochelle would kill me if she knew I was telling you this." She furtively looked at her phone. Mr. Pax, Arthur, we are not exactly fae, but we are not exactly human either. Have you heard stories of the Zorya Sisters, also known as the morning and evening stars?" I nodded. "That is what some of the slavic people call Sonya and I. Our real names are Zvezda Danica, Danni, and Vechernyaya, Sonya. My other two sisters; Rochelle is Snegurochka, the Snow Maiden, and Allie is Rusalka in our native tongue."

"Rusalka? Do you mean the spirit of a drowned woman who wants to drown other men?" I asked.

She lightly smiled, "That is what the Imperialists want you to believe. No, Rusalka was honored as a fertility goddess in the time before Pyotr Velikiy and his devil, Nikon, came and 'tamed the wild Rusian spirit' with the Catholic Church."

St. Nikon, born Nikita Minin, was a Mordovian monk that taught Pyotr Velikiy, also known as Peter the Great. Pyotr helped elect

Nikon to become the Patriarch of Moscow and instituted massive reforms in the Russian Orthodox Church, which caused a giant schism between the reformists and the *staroobryádtsy*, or Old Believers. Because of this reform, rural believers still celebrated *Semik*, the spring festival to this day. Some traditions cannot be taken away, even with Communism. I once read that there was a group of the Old Believers that were found living in a remote village in Siberia during the Brezhnev era. The leaders had no idea what to do with them, because they had read the reports of Old Believer monks that lit their entire monastery on fire with them inside because they didn't want to change their ways.

I looked at Danni, she looked suddenly much older than she appeared. It was as if she had aged dramatically in the past few minutes while revealing her secrets to me. "If Rusalka, or Allie as you are calling her, isn't found, doesn't that just mean a longer winter? I guess that just means Punxatawni Phil gets to sleep a bit longer, right?" I was trying to lighten up the mood.

Danni's look turned hauntingly dark. "The last time Rusalka and Snegurochka had an argument, Rusalka didn't do her job to the best of her abilities and many people died. I believe you historians call it "The Little Ice Age?" Many historians know that during the Middle Ages, around the time of the Bubonic Plague outbreak, the winters were more harsh. The population dropped by about one-hundred thousand. Longer more harsh winters meant crops weren't producing properly. Then the plague hit in 1347 and lasted until 1351 and more people died. Some historians say the Little Ice Age lasted until the mid 1800s in some parts of Europe, but it wasn't as bad as between the fourteenth and fifteenth centuries.

"Okay, so Rusalka goes missing and we're looking at a possible full blown Ice Age?" I pondered out loud.

"That and when Snegurochka doesn't sleep she gets really bitchy. At least Sonya and I can sleep regularly, but when Snegurochka and Rusalka are tending to their duties, they cannot sleep." This created a whole set of problems that I had not thought about. If Rusalka isn't found, the Ice Age is the least of our concerns. Food supplies will dwindle rapidly, or food production would have to be moved from the fertile belt to being produced around the equator. That means less rainforests, which produce the vast majority of our oxygen supply. Let alone the shortage of habitable areas to live. North America, Europe and the majority of Asia would have to move to more tropical climates. Living spaces would become at a premium cost and there would be billions homeless and starving. It would almost be a mass extinction of not only humans, but other living plants and animals, globally.

"Well, shit. That complicates things." I poked at my spaghetti as we sat in silence. Both of us had lost our appetite for the moment. "Alright, not that this hasn't been fun and all, but I need to go check out that club and figure out if there is a bigger plot afoot." I signaled the waitress and asked for boxes and the check. She offered us complimentary ice cream to go and I shuddered thinking about possibly never being warm again. We politely declined.

Chapter Seventeen

Interlude the 13th
A Fairy Story

It has been told time and time again about the dangers of dealings with the Fae, or Faeries. Especially on certain nights of the week or in specific areas around the globe, it is cautioned from entering their realm. Entrances could be found in rings of mushrooms, hills in the countryside, watery caves or in thick bramble patches.

Typically, mortals would want to steer clear of these areas because the fae do not have the same moral compass that has been instilled into people due to religion. There have been many tales of the dangers of having any kind of dealing with the Fae. From making deals, to taking prized possessions from them, to even partying with the Fae. It is often said, though that one has never been to a party like a Fae party, because a Fae party doesn't stop.

Take for instance the tale of Kate Crackernuts. This Scottish account tells about two sisters, one beautiful and one cunning. Kate and Anne were princesses, sisters bound by marriage. The queen was jealous of her husband's daughter, Anne because Anne was the beautiful daughter. Through trickery with a hen-wife, a British wyld woman, Anne literally lost her head and the queen replaced it with a goat's head, as you do. The sisters fled and found themselves in a neighboring kingdom with two sons. One was healthy and handsome, the other was sickly, but still handsome, in a Gothic kind of way.

Kate, the cunning sister made a deal with the king that they would help the sickly son if he gave them a roof over their heads. Kate stayed up the first night and at the stroke of midnight, the sickly son rose from his bed, just fine. Kate stuck by his side as he saddled his horse and rode led by moonlight to a hill with a door on the side. He knocked, it was opened, Kate hid and watched him party all night like an emo on ecstasy. At times, he would fall down of sheer exhaustion, the Fae would fan him, give him water and he would get up to dance again. He went home after the cock crowed the morning sun to rise.

This went on for three nights, but the second night Kate found out about a wand that would make her sister Anne beautiful again. The third night she found out about a bird that if the sick prince ate three bites of it, would cure his dancing sickness. Needless to say, Kate and the sick prince were wed after the spell was lifted and Anne and the handsome prince were wed after she regained her natural beauty.

There are many other accounts of people having a wasting sickness that resembled tuberculosis. The rational explanation back in the day was dancing all night with the Fae. It might be the best explanation over a bacterial infection that eventually kills someone by coughing up blood.

Chapter Eighteen
Is It Loud Here or Am I Just Old?

Claud pulled up to the curb at the club. In purple neon, the words Liquid Dreams dripped above a red door. I had asked Danni if she wanted to come with me, but she told me she had to work the night shift at the stable she and Sonja own. With a heavy heart I had to bid her goodnight. We hugged tightly as she teared up and reiterated the need to find Allie. I really wanted to kiss her right there, but I felt the timing wasn't right. We started to pull apart from our hug and she leaned up to softly place a tender kiss on my lower lip before turning away. My head swam with unspoken possibilities and electric desires. Those thoughts carried me from downtown to Broad Ripple.

Originally founded in 1837, the village of Broad Ripple is one of the seven cultural centers in Indy. With Butler University nearby, the cultural scene went from just artistic to a thriving nightlife. The latest and greatest clubs were either opened up downtown or in Broad Ripple. Everyone who lived in Indy, at one point in their life, had visited The Vogue or Alley Cat Lounge. They were staples from the 80s forward for all kinds of dancing kings and queens. The Vogue also held regular concerts from all the popular music artists, from Debbie Gibson to the Rolling Stones. If you never made a trip to The Vogue, you were basically shunned.

It wasn't always like that, though. Originally, the nightclub opened as a movie theater in the 1930s. For the next thirty years or so, it was the premier place to preview panoramic pictures in Indianapolis. Then it became a porno theater from 1970 to 1978. At the beginning of

'78, The Vogue was reopened as a nightclub and has stayed that way ever since. That means mysterious fluids of all kinds have been on the floor since it opened.

Liquid Dreams though, was off the beaten path. Most of the clubs and bars are on the main strip of College Ave. There are some in hidden alcoves and second floors of old shop fronts. I know there used to be a cigar bar hidden in plain sight. There was no sign, other than an arrow that pointed to a stairwell. When you ascended the stairs, the solid wood door had a simple sign of hours. If it was unlocked, it was open. If it was open, you were greeted with the sounds of soft jazz, lower mood lighting, a spirits bar and the delicious smell of high priced cigars.

Claud opened the door for me and I gave him a slight nod. We had worked out a signal on the drive over, if things got a bit too hairy for me in the club by myself. I walked up to the door and before reaching the handle, it opened by itself. They must have some kind of video feed and automatic opening mechanism. Outwardly, I was the picture of calm, cool suavité; inside, I was a mess. I mean, sure I knew how to kick ass and hold my own, but I had no idea what I was walking into.

The entire building buzzed with magic. Even though I couldn't use the mystical arts, I could still sense it. Some people say it is more of an electrical buzz, for me it felt like an overwhelming pressure over my chest. It wasn't a bad pressure like a very large person sitting on it. The pressure was closer to having a bunch of cats sitting on my chest and purring very loudly. The brick entryway only had one bare bulb dimly lit and ended in a purple door, the same shade as the sign outside. I walked to the purple door and the front door closed as the inner door swung inward. The first few beats of typical techno music crept to my ears and massaged its way to my bones. It was slightly euphoric.

The room was lit by several candles in sconces on the walls that were covered in an old Victorian style wallpaper that was a red and green diamond harlequin style pattern accentuated with copper lines. An old style coat check door stood to the left and a ticket window was to my right draped in red velvet curtains, either of which was completely dark a few inches inside the portals.

"Mr. Pax, I see you received your invitation," a hidden voice came from my right. I turned to the ticket booth and a figure materialized from the darkness. Ghostly pale with dark hair, the man wore attire fitting the Victorian theme. His eyes were outlined with dark mascara and his lips were stained a dark purple. Great, another Hollywood fanger fan. Vampire wannabes really irritate me because they think they are all trendy and chic. Granted not all of the vampire lore is what Bram Stoker and Hollywood make you think they are. Vampire lore comes from all corners of the globe. Most original European lore states that vampires were ruddy in complexion and bloated, basically the exact opposite of how they are portrayed now.

"What kind of club is this? The only thing that was in the invitation was a website with this address?" I tried to keep my tone casual and aloof.

The ticket agent smiled and showed an impressive set of prosthetic dentures that made his canines look like something from an Anne Rice film. "This is a premiere night club that combines the best of old world charm and new world sensuality. It is both a dance club for the younger crowd and an old style burlesque, with shows every hour on the hour. We offer the best spirits and cigars for our discerning clientele, such as yourself, Mr. Pax. If you care, you can leave your coat with the lovely young lady across the room from me. For you, there is never going to be a cover charge because of your celebrity status." He ended with a flourish, a bow and disappeared back into the shadows.

I turned around to see a tall, but pixyish brunette pop out of thin air. Her smile was from ear to ear framed by her plush lips. Her light brown skin was warm and inviting. I found myself compelled to start taking off my coat as I walked the three steps it took to cross the hall. She was wearing a low cut, off the shoulder black and grey pin striped dress that did nothing to hide her very visible assets. A waist cincher black corset helped emphasize her hourglass figure. As I handed her my coat I noticed that even though her mouth was warm and friendly, her deep brown eyes didn't carry her smile and before I could ask her anything, the doors to the club opened and the candlelit corridor was flooded with a myriad of flashing and strobing lights and my ears were fully assaulted with the deep throbbing of the sensual music.

My unvoiced question went to the back of my mind as I reflexively went through the new portal. Strobe lights switched colors slowly in time with the sounds of house music being piped in from hidden speakers. The Victorian theme continued in the main room. The walls were covered in wood panelling that went up about three feet and topped with striped pink and light green wallpaper. There were wall sconces with candles interspersed evenly to add to the ambiance. To the left was an old style bar, straight out of the Old West, complete with a set of Texas Longhorns hanging over the mirrored backboard. There were a couple of dozen tables scattered around a large dance floor, which was covered with writhing bodies semingly in midcoitus as they musically swived.

Just beyond the dance floor was a raised stage framed with red and blue velvet curtains. Framed with marquee lights, it lay empty, but it looked like quite a show had happened on it recently. There was about a metric ton of glitter and confetti littering the area. I saw an older gentleman step from stage left with a big push broom and started the Herculean task of cleaning it. Hopefully, he won't reroute the canal through the club like Heracles did with the Augean stables. He looked very weary and worn down, so I doubted he could.

Sidebar: I know most of you are asking, isn't the demigod's name Hercules? Well, yes, however that is his Roman name. In Greek mythology, he was named Heracles by Zeus after his wife Hera, the goddess of matrimonial faithfulness. Kind of funny that she was married to the most promiscuous cad of the entire lot. According to popular myth, Zeus had a dalliance with the mortal Alcmene, who according to Hesiod was tall, dark and strikingly beautiful with eyes that rivaled Aphrodite. The problem with this dalliance, other than the obvious cheating on Hera, Zeus disguised himself as Alcmene's husband Amphytrion. Who came home later that night and impregnated her with his offspring. There Alcmene was, giving birth to twins from two different fathers. When Hera found out about this latest dalliance, she was understandably pissed especially when Zeus declared that a child born on a specific date and inherit the throne of the High King. Hera had Ilithyia, goddess of childbirth, to delay the birth of the twins and another child was born. The twins were born and Amphytrion's son was named Iphicles and Zeus' son was named after his goddess in matrimony, Heracles, to appease her wrath. It did not, but I digress.

The right side of the room had more private booths with red and blue velvet curtains to offer a more intimate sitting area, in which half of the shades were drawn. I moved to head toward the bar, as the song was winding down and fading out. The lights stopped rotating and strobing and dimmed almost to complete darkness. Two spotlights from opposite ends of the stage shattering the near darkness. The curtain parted and a finely bespoke leg broke the curtain line in the direct center of the stage. The curtains parted enough to let out a man wearing an outfit that looked like something worn by P.T. Barnum, a red tuxedo with tails, white vest, dark blue bow tie, black pants with a yellow stripe down the side; complete with a silk tophat, white gloves and walking stick.

"Ladies and gentlemen!' He swept the cane out to the side, removed his hat and did a short, curt bow. As he popped back up, the crowd roared with approval. "Thank you for coming and visiting my humble establishment. It is only with kind patronage, we are able to keep the *Dream* alive." The audience laughed and cheered at his word play. I just groaned inwardly. "As you know, we here at Liquid Dreams want to build a haven for the lost and condemned souls to dance the nights away and be entertained with the finest burlesque numbers that money can buy." More cheers. "Manager, please bring up the house lights a bit so our fair patrons can find their way to a seat, because for this next number, you will want to be seated. You men might find it a bit <ahem> difficult to stand and women might as well have 'slippery when wet' signs in front of their tables."

He disappeared back into the curtain. Various catcalls and whistles heralded the patrons as they quickly shuffled to their seats in the brighter room. Waitresses appeared from beside the bar to weave their way around the tables asking for drink orders. It was a finely tuned ballet. I could see that the waitresses had similar placid looks on their faces, like the coat check lady, smiles that didn't seem to reach their eyes. That was mildly disturbing.

I worked my way to a seat near the bar at a table with only two chairs. One of the Stepford waitresses quickly came over and asked me to follow her. "Our VIPs have assigned booths, Mr. Pax." That took me by surprise. I mean, I know I am really popular in the world of academia, but not in the rest of the world. I noticed the curtains that were previously closed were opened, but still too dark to see well enough inside. "Please feel free to order anything. Our bar is fully stocked with everything you could desire." Her voice was too damn chipper for a place like this.

I ordered a GnT, top shelf gin, chilled tonic water with a squeeze of blood orange, rolled not shaken or stirred. Rolling a drink basically pours it from one cup to another, which mixes it nicely and doesn't lose the fizziness from the tonic. She nodded and whisked away to the bar, which had four tenders doing their own free form jazz dance prepping the multitude of drink requests.

I scanned the room with the other patrons, it was a generous mix of ages, skin tones, hair colors and dress styles from emo to club rat to business casual. The more affluent patrons were closer to the stage and I could only catch glimpses from the other VIPs, which were dressed like they belonged in an opera house, not a nightclub in Broad Ripple. The room was slightly hazy from the cigar and pipe tobacco smoke that circled lazily in the lights with a slight blue haze. I could see that the smoke spiraled upward and disappeared in hidden vents.

The waitress dropped off my drink, a freshly packed pipe and a box of wooden matches. "Compliments of the house, Mr. Pax. The owner thought you might enjoy this golden cavendish with your drink. He said it matched perfectly with the blood orange," and went to the next booth to deliver more drinks and other pairings of tobacco products. A fanfare blasted from the speakers, a la Muppet style and the crowd fell silent. I picked up the highball glass and sniffed it. Holy fuck this smelled divine. I took a sip as the Emcee came back out. The flavor of the sweet blood orange juice and earthy gin, mixed together on my tongue hitting all of the flavor sensors at once. It was the perfect mix and the perfect temperature. I next picked up the pipe and sniffed the tobacco; the orange and raisin smell pulled into my nostrils and mixed with the drink. Just from the smell, yes it would match perfectly.

I lit the pipe and started relaxing with my drink and burning tobacco as the Emcee said, "*Mesdames et Messieurs*, tonight you are in for a very special treat. We get to have a glimpse behind the Iron Curtain of the former Soviet Union. This lovely, risque Russian *dyevushka* is here to tantalize your senses with her fiery spirit and stormy looks. She is only around for a limited time, so without further ado, I will call the smouldery siren to sing and sway for your pleasure." As he slipped to stage right he finished his introduction, "Please, get your tips and applause ready for The Mistress of Storms, RrrrrrrrrusalkAAaaaa!"

I almost spit my drink out and dropped the pipe when the curtain parted and the spotlights lit up Allie Zvezdochka, formerly known as Rusalka aka, my meal ticket. The room started spinning with seeing her as I felt a panic attack come out of nowhere. I hadn't had a full blown panic attack in about a decade, but I knew that if I didn't get it under control, I would black out. The waitress was walking past me on her way back to the bar. I tried to say something and my mouth completely dried up and only an odd grunting noise came out. I tried to raise my arm to wave her down, but it was a lead weight tied to the table. The panic rose in me as my heart sped up. I could almost feel my blood pressure rising. Darkness started creeping into my whirling vision. I didn't know if it was the room or just my eyes, which were still able to dart around. I saw a shadow darken the left side of my curtained booth and the Cheshire grinning face of the owner came into view as I slid silently into the darkness of oblivion. And this is how I die...

Chapter Nineteen

December 1992

The frosted crystals hung in the air, not moving for a fraction of a second as the heated carbon dioxide mixed with internal moisture came out of my mouth. I studied the slowly expanding cloud as it ballooned out and filled the space in front of my face. Every time I blew out that first breath of the day, I imagined I was a wizard from some fantasy novel sitting and smoking his pipe to relax after a long day of conjuring and experimentations.

It was the first day of the holiday break during my senior year of high school. I had been looking forward to the welcome break in my scholastic studies so I could focus on more of the mystical studies that Felix had been tutoring me. It was just excruciatingly cold in my room. I wrapped myself in my blanket tighter and rolled over to go back to sleep, but my bladder reminded me why I woke up in the first place.

I really didn't want to break the burrito of warmth I had going on in my sleeping bag. Yes, we had regular blankets and comforters in the house, but I really liked sleeping in my bag. I also really didn't want to open my eyes. I had stayed up late playing a dungeon crawl video game on my computer to help celebrate the end of the semester. In the wee hours of the morning something outside my window caught my attention. I paused my game long enough to glance out my window to see it starting to snow.

This was the first snow of the year and I loved the first snow of the year. I shifted my focus from killing pixels to watching the fat, crystallized water slowly drifting past my window. It was easy to roll my basic office style chair from my desk to the window, which I did, gleefully. I shut off my desk lamp, rolled over to the window and opened it wide. The wind wasn't blowing very much so I didn't have to worry about the cold night air blowing in my room. I sat in awe watching the flurry grow into a downright squall for about an hour. There was about a foot accumulated before I decided to turn in for the night.

I drifted off to sleep thinking about the *Emerald Tablet* of Hermes. Felix had taught me about the tablet early on in my tutelage because it held the main tenets of the Believers. It was not very long, but had a profound impact on the studies of many cultures throughout history. It was also the reason that I woke up freezing. I had left the window open a crack.

I rose, after much debate, to close the window, put on socks, wrapped myself in my fluffy, red house robe and relieved myself. Thankfully, mom had to work the early shift at the diner she was currently waiting at and I had the house to myself.

Relief achieved, I shuffled into the kitchen to see if she had left me any coffee. The dear sweet saint did, and it was still hot enough to warm me, but not scalding hot enough to burn my tongue. I shuffled back to my room with the coffee to start the day. I really didn't feel like going out in the cold, but I had to go and visit Felix. Even though school was not in session, Schule was still in Session. He was German after all.

It took me a bit to wait for the bus to come pick me up to trek across the city to his house. While standing at the stop, I looked at the beauty of the untouched snow on most of the lawns in my neighborhood. Thankfully, there was enough cloud cover to tone down the blaringly white of the fresh powder, so I didn't have to squint too much. It was quiet. Even with a major street nearby, I didn't really hear the shushing of tires on wet roads that I normally heard. I loved the first snow of the year. I know I have mentioned this before, but you just don't understand unless you have lived in a place that gets snow every winter.

The banging of screen doors and laughter of children broke me out of my reverence. The neighborhood kids had emerged from their wooden and plaster filled cocoons. Brightly colored in their winter attire and holding their sleds, they all had one thing in mind, to be the first kid to slide down Suicide Hill. It was a badge of honor in my neighborhood.

The bus pulled up shortly after a few impromptu snowball fights and much rough housing by the kids and I left the scene of nostalgic tumult. Only a half hour later, I was at Felix's house in Fountain Square. By car it would normally take less than ten minutes, but public transportation and inclement weather made for slow driving. In the summers I would just ride my bike along Pleasant Run Parkway to get there, but it was a bit too chilly and the snow was a bit too fresh to comfortably ride by bicycle.

I jumped off the bus near the heart of Fountain Square. While it doesn't officially have boundaries delineated, it is about one square mile. The main features of the neighborhood are the convergences of three main roads Prospect Street, Shelby Street and the diagonally running Virginia Avenue, as well as the fountain that sits in the middle-ish of the three streets.

The fountain was originally built in 1889, when local business owners thought to build it as a way station for farmers to water their horses to and from the downtown market square. It had fallen to disrepair, as did the rest of a once thriving entertainment and cultural center. Lately, they were in the beginnings of revitalizing the area so it was kind of under construction. It seems like everything in the 90s was always under construction, but this is the world we live in and these are the hands we're given.

I wandered past the statue of the Pioneer Family and didn't even think twice about it because it was just a fountain in the middle of winter, so it wasn't even turned on. The wind was a bit cutting as it wrapped itself around the movie theater and I bundled myself up a bit tighter, but I knew the walk wasn't too far. I soldiered on through the fresh snow. Not too many people wanted to be out today, which was fine for me.

It took me a few minutes of plodding to reach Felix's house which was a nice older German built brick longhouse. No front porch to speak of, but it was sturdy, warm, has two stories with a fully finished basement and an attic. It was perfect for hiding secrets because it looked just like the rest of the neighborhood.

Felix told me that German immigrants came and settled here in the post Civil War era and this neighborhood sprung up overnight, practically. Most of the houses were this style, not much imagination, but inexpensive to build and sturdy enough to last through the harsh Indiana winters. A hundred years later and the winters were not as harsh due to global warming and the hole in the ozone, but the houses were as warm and cozy as ever.

I rounded the corner to see an ambulance parked near Felix's house. My heart leapt into my throat and I started running. My biggest fear was coming to fruition. Felix was going to be dead and he won't continue my training and with him not having any heirs his property would be destroyed and the secrets of the Believers would be found out and Felix is standing on his porch looking next door.

Wait, what?

I slowed down as I reached his chain link fence and all of my fears melted away when I saw his bright friendly eyes smiling at me with melancholy.

"My neighbor Mr. Schoenvetter passed last night," he offered with a sad smile. "Why were you running, Art? You know you can't get rid of me that easily." We both laughed, mine was a bit more nervous than I wanted to admit.

"Did you think I was running for you? I always jog in the fresh snow," I hoped he bought my fabrication, but I knew he didn't.

"Feh. Arnold was always a pain in my ass. He let his walnut trees grow out of control and they would drop their nuts everywhere. I asked him politely for decades to trim them down, but he never did, the stubborn bastard. Ah well, now he can drive St. Michael nuts with his nut problems." Felix smiled and turned to head inside the house. "Oh you can start your lesson out here since you want to go running around in the snow like a crazy yeti or something like that." He pointed to the shovel on the porch and went inside without another word.

I took a few minutes to catch my breath and watch as the paramedics came out of a house similar to Felix's with the gurney. Mr. Schoenvetter was completely covered with a blanket and strapped down as they traversed down the three steps to the sidewalk still covered in snow. The only thing that had disturbed the pristine scene was the footprints between the door and the ambulance.

I had never been this close to a dead body before and oddly it didn't disturb me as much as I thought it would. Granted, I have always had a healthy appreciation for death and was never really afraid of it.

Blame my youth, my bravado or just naivete, but I didn't fear death nor really felt sad when I received news of someone passing. It was just a natural part of the human life cycle.

The bulky paramedics wrestled with getting the wheels down to roll him to the back of the meat wagon and somehow one of them slipped on the snow enough to jar the gurney. The recently deceased's hand fell out of the blanket that they failed to properly swaddle him in. It was pale grey, which was odd to me because the last time I saw his hand, it was very pinkish and covered with white hairs. Sure the hair was still there, but it just didn't look like his hand at all. The door was shut from the inside, probably by his wife, I'm guessing.

A couple of swear words and they got him righted again. It wasn't easy to move him in the snow and slush that was forming around the back of the running ambulance, but they got him up there with a few more bumps, curses and left without ceremony. Sure the lights were on, but no siren. I walked to Felix's three by three porch that has three steps, he told me it was a magic porch, because three threes was a perfect magic number, grabbed the shovel and got to work going from the front of the house to the sidewalk.

After about a solid half hour of scraping, tossing and grunting, my back and arms were kind of on fire, but I was just getting started. Out of respect, I kept shovelling down the street and up Mr. Schoevetter's walkway. It was the least I could do since he was always kind to me and gave me giant paper bags full of Black walnuts, which were my favorite treat, albeit a bit messy to break into. He taught me the best way to crack them open and not stain my fingers black from the shell. I always preferred the smell and robust flavor over the kind of dull English variety. As I slowly crept forward, shove, scrape, toss, shove, scrape, toss, I saw something in the snow. It was nearby the spot that he was jarred and his lifeless hand fell out. I stooped over and found a black walnut lying on the white snow. I picked it up and smiled. It was as if he left me one final gift before leaving his home forever.

While I was lost in memory of walnuts and stories from the past, I missed that his front door opened. I looked up to see a younger version of Mr. Schoenvetter standing there holding out a steaming mug.

"I'm Arnold's son, David. You must be Arthur." I nodded. "My Papa told me about you and your love for walnuts. This cup of cocoa is for you and so is my thanks. I don't know if I could have shoveled as fast as you did. It's kind of difficult for me to move quickly anymore." He looked down at his leg, which was encased in a metal and leather cage. In all the time I have been coming over here I never saw David, nor his leg brace.

"It's nothing, Mr. Schoenvetter. I usually do both walks when it snows. Even though Mr. Blau and Mr. Schoenvetter didn't always see eye to eye, they were friends and don't let him," I pointed my thumb to Felix's house, "tell you any different." I took the warm cocoa and returned a smile in thanks.

"I'll let you to it then, Arthur. You can leave the mug on the porch, if you want. No need to bring it in. we can take it from there. There's a lot of planning we need to do and Mama isn't really in the mood for company. But hey, as long as someone in the family owns the house you're welcome to as many walnuts as you want." David gave a tight grimace, waved and closed the door as I heard wailing coming from somewhere in the house.

I know they were married for seventy years and at the sound of Mrs. Schoenvetter's unbridled grief, I had to catch a few of my tears as I sipped the delicious hot potion. Death certainly had a way of affecting people in different ways. I looked at the death gift he had left me and knew he was going to be in a better place.

"Life certainly has a way of giving you lessons even when you aren't expecting them, eh boy?" I looked up to see Felix wearing his parka and headed up the walkway. He looked at the walnut in my hand through blurry eyes. "That old bastard never tended his trees, but those nuts were some of the best I have ever eaten. Sometimes, you don't have to tend and constantly fuss over things to get the best results. Kind of like my friendship with Arnold. We never really sat around the cracker barrel and swapped stories, but his wife makes the best walnut cake you have ever eaten and we were always willing to lend a hand when things got rough. Even though I never married and had kids of my own, I watched David and his sister Ingrid grow up playing in those damn trees and it was fine for me. I remember when David fell out from a branch taller than his bedroom and smashed his leg to smithereens. His parents were away and Ingrid was in charge, but it didn't stop me from scooping up the boy and taking him to the hospital. Doctors did everything they could to fix it, but there was only so much they could do. That's why he is all strapped up like that, if you were wondering." He stopped to take in a big breath and let out a heartfelt sigh. "I'm going to pay my respects to the family. If you want to knock off today and enjoy life, go ahead. This is your lesson for the day: Sometimes it pays to not cultivate too much. This matters in plants and in life. Go, enjoy being young."

I handed him the now empty mug, he shuffled inside and I finished the last few feet of snow before I put the shovel back on Felix's porch. I didn't want to go home, just yet but I also didn't want to hang around here, so I headed to a nearby cafe and just sat rolling the walnut on the table for a few hours before heading home.

Chapter Twenty
Date: Unknown

The watery apocalypse dream came back, just like before. Me, in a field. Next to a pond. Creepy skeletons start coming out of the water. The trees, the wind, the leaves, all of it exactly the same as before. The souls started to come after me again, but this time, I wasn't frozen in place. I could at least move my head and upper torso to look around. I already knew how this dream was to end, so I didn't worry about the souls attacking me. I just knew I needed to see where the deadly death ray of damning the dead came from and dammit, I was going to find out. I turned as best I could to look behind me and saw a silhouette near the tree line. The sun was rising behind the trees beyond my shadowy savior. I could hear the souls coming closer as before, but I kept my eyes on the new figure in the dream.

A new thought came to my head. Is this the afterlife? Am I to be stuck in this Apocalyptic nightmare of the souls escaping to wreak havoc on the Mortal Plane? I heard a car horn blare across the field. I turned to see from whence it came.

Did I just think from whence it came? The hell is going on here? I turned back to the shadowed figure and saw a red glow in their hands. Expanding, like the sun breaking the horizon, the figure did not reflect the light, it was as if the mystery person was made out of antilight. That's nit the roght werd. Wait. The Hell is Going On Here?

The light grew brytter and brytter as my thothts grew harder and hardER to hold onto. The wirld became red light. Red light. Red. Rrrrrrrrr

I am cold. Where is my blanket? My bankie. My blu blu bankie? Mama! I fursty! Ma MA! Why is the world so blurry? What is that tune playing with the spinning toys that are just out of my reach? It is SO bright! Why can't anyone understand me? AAAAAAAAAAAAAAAAAAA! Back in warmth. The person who calls itself Mommy is hungry. I am hungry. Ugh I need to stretch my legs, it is so cramped in here. Stretch! Ooh, she is pushing on me from outside my safe place. I hear laughing and deep voice and a high voice. Wheee-ooooh! Wheee-ooooh! Wheee-ooooh!

There's that damn car horn again. I am floating in a lake. There are lots of people laughing and splashing around me. I wish they would just shut the hell up and let me float in peace. I know I am getting close to the diving platform, but I also know I can still stand up and reach the sandy bottom. Maybe I will go ask Mom to go to the petting zoo and feed the baby deer. Faun? Doe? Buck? A tisket a tasket, I lost my yellow basket.

I am so damn cold. I still don't know what happened to my favorite bankie. Have you seen it Mommy? You know it's blue with the silky edges. It feels so good to snuggle up with. She was morning and I was night time. Wheee-ooooh!

I rolled over to kiss whatever her name was. She was hawt and Chuck thought he had an ounce of a chance with her. I mean, he's no smooth talker like me. I know the secret, honeyed words that can lure the young women into bed, even if I am old and have only one eye. Fuck, I rock that dam eyepatch. I rick that ipatch. I patch that rockeye. Rock...

and roll. Techno. I get knocked down, but I can get up again. Thou art ne'er to keep me down. Down. I dropped my pipe. It fell down to the floor. I should pick it up and check to see if it's still lit. Wait, wasn't there a drink too? WHEEEE-OOOOOH!

I am cold, shivering, my head hurts, another car blast and red fucking light. That fucking red goddamn light is so fucking bright.

I reached to pull my blanket up and couldn't move my arms. There was a screaming sound intermittently interrupted by a horn blaring. "It looks like he is coming to." Beeping. Is that a heart monitor? "Mr. Pax?! Can you hear me?"

I didn't want to open my eyes. It was too damn bright. Someone forced my eye open and flashed an extremely bright light in it. Then the offender did the same to my other eye. Did they call me Mr. Pax? Who the hell is that? I tried to open my mouth, but it felt like there was a hose or tube or something in it. My nose was being blasted with cold, uncomfortable air. My heart leapt in speed. I couldn't move, people were poking and prodding me. I felt a sharp pain and something was cutting off circulation on my left arm. My right hand was in intense pain as I tried to move it around.

"His heart rate is elevating. BP is rising, finally. We are at 93 over 62; heart rate is 94 BPM. Welcome back, Mr. Pax. Try not to move too much. We have you stabilized for now, but we're not out of the woods, yet. Try not to speak, we had to intubate you." More sirens, more honking. I tried to open my eyes. Just a little at a time, but fuck me it hurt.

The world was blurry and everything hurt. I tried to move again and nothing. "Please do not try to move, Mr. Pax. We had to strap you down to a board. You look like you were in an accident, but there was no automobile nearby. Do you remember anything? Blink once for yes, twice for no." I tried to blink twice. It felt like my lids were weighed down with giant feathery fake eyelashes. And before you ask, yes I have worn feathery fake eyelashes that weighed a ton. I was young, alone and bored. Shut up.

The EMT tried to ask me a few more questions, but I couldn't open my eyes, I felt physically exhausted and had no fucking clue as to what had led me to be in this state. The last thing I remember was snippets of going on a date with the Divine Danni. I was using every trick I know to recall any detail and before I knew it, they were pulling up to a hospital. The rig stopped and the doors flew open and everything was a blur and my senses were overwhelmed again which led me back down the black hole of unconsciousness.

I awoke again in a much darker place. The incessant beeping of hospital machinery was the first thing I heard. The general noises of a busy hospital in the background. I opened my eyes to take in my surroundings. I didn't feel any restraints on me, so I lifted my head. There was still a tube in my mouth, so I felt around for the call button. It was easily within reach. One of those new fangled ones with TV and bed control. I raised the head of the bed which set off a new alarm. A nurse came in and saw my eyes opened and called for the attending. Three people in various colors of scrubs rushed in asking rapid fire questions. I pointed to the tube and the doctor called for a prep tray to remove it. Between all of the hubbub and jargon, I caught that I was a John Doe, had been brought in found behind a building near downtown, looked like I was in a bar fight or a hit and run accident, all of this was divulged as they were taking of the medical tape around my mouth and nose. None of this made sense to me, but I also didn't remember anything after the date.

"On one, two, three." the tube came sliding out of my throat. I felt like I was going to lose my stomach contents, thankfully there was nothing in it. The dry heaves hurt, though. Every inch of my body hurt; felt like it was one giant bruise. I didn't see or feel any casts on me, not even a neck brace. Sure there was a catheter in my left arm and a BP cuff on the other, but nothing else.

"Where?" I was able to croak out. My throat felt like someone had fed me a sandpaper sandwich and gave me some salt water to drink.

"Sir, try not to talk. The EMTs had to intubate you in the ambulance. It looked like someone had crushed your larynx. You are at Wishard Hospital. It looks like they found you at…" He swiped the screen on his tablet. A tablet? I guess that's more green friendly than a ton of papers being used on multiple charts. "…oh looks like you were found near The Pasta Place. Does that mean anything to you?"

I nodded and whispered, "Date."

"You were found without any identification or a cell phone, three days ago. You have been in a medically induced coma to give the swelling in your brain time to reduce. I have to admit, it was a bit touch and go, for a while, Mr?" The doctor paused again waiting for an answer.

I took a deep breath, which hurt to croak out, "Pax, Arthur Pax," which hurt to say. The doctor started typing on the tablet and looked up.

"Arthur Pax, as in the author?" I nodded cautiously. The young attending physician's face lit up. "I have read every single book you have written. Your book describing Satanic witchcraft as simply ancient cultic practices was mind blowing! It, it was crazy to see the exact paper trail you used. I mean, the Catholic Church, man." He was practically stumbling over his words by the end of his outburst. He took a breath to calm himself. "I apologize, Mr. Pax. It has been a dream of mine to talk to you to pick your brain on many subjects, but you are my patient and I am Dr. Jones. Now that we know who you are, is there anyone we can call for you?"

I nodded and simply said "Chuck Silver." I didn't want to worry my mom, yet and I knew Chuck would help break the news to her gently.

"And how would we get a hold of him?" He was tapping the information on the tablet.

"Phonebook. Owns a business." With each breath I was getting more and more weary, but something struck me from what he said. "Three days?" I inquired.

"Yes, Mr. Pax. Do you remember anything about how you were attacked?" I shook my head as a tear came to my eye. Normally, I am not the type of guy to cry but this was fucking overwhelming. I don't think Danni would have done anything to me, but I cannot figure out what the fuck happened. There is literally nothing in my expansive memory after we met for dinner. I can remember my first day of kindergarten. I can remember what I was wearing the first day that I saw Sarah Spelunknick in a bikini after we turned fifteen. Damn what a hottie, I wonder what she's doing now? Many memories came up with ease, but nothing after Danni and I met.

I took a deep breath as the sobs wracked my chest. Dr. Jones lightly patted my right hand as the BP cuff started to inflate again. "In some cases of blunt force trauma to the head, amnesia is often a side effect. It could be temporary or permanent, depending how much trauma there was to your brain while it was swollen. For now, we will contact Mr. Silver and since you are awake, we will meet as a team to figure out the best steps for care." He mumbled something to himself as he tapped more on the tablet, nodded his head and said his goodbye.

The entire team left as another more matronly nurse came in to clean up the tube and tape. She gave me the rundown on the call button and offered me some ice chips to help numb the sore throat. I nodded my head and she made a retreat after checking on the amount of saline in the IV bag.

I lay on the bed trying not to have a panic attack. Missing memory is one of my biggest fears. I have worked very hard at retaining information throughout my life. Sure I might forget someone's birthday or one of their kid's names, but when it came to the important things, I had an impeccable memory. I guess the best description of how my memory works is like a wet sponge. The important things soak in but the nonessential bit of information, just kind of leak through or roll off the top.

I was restless and exhausted at the same time, so I lifted the bed a bit more and turned on the television. The evening news had just started on CBS. The reporters said it was the 21st and Thanksgiving was less than a week away. They were even doing a countdown until the lighting ceremony and another until Black Friday. The snow had started again and didn't look like it was going to end. But the big story was continuing coverage about an attack in Jerusalem that happened on the 18th. I guess with all the research and drinking I had been doing recently, I had been rather negligent on the current state of affairs. About halfway through the recap, my room phone rang.

I looked to the right to find where the offending noise was coming from. It was within reach so I picked up the handle and before I could put it to my ear, Chuck was already going back and forth between yelling and almost crying for joy. He had already told my mom, Claud had been in contact with him and had been looking every day for me, Rochelle had contacted him as well. Even Declan and Champagne had started a sexy Little People search party. He said something about a club, Liquid Dreams and they were all coming up with nothing. The police were alerted this morning and he was so glad I was alive and how was I doing?

I let him breathe for a few seconds before I told him I was hurting and can't remember much. I sounded like a septigeneric chain smoker from Jersey, but I was able to croke it all out. He gasped at the sound of my voice and then the phone made a weird clicking noise. Chuck said hold on, apparently he had another call coming in. He switched back after a few seconds. "Your mom is on her way."

Chapter 21
The Gang's All Here
November 20

I knew I only had about 20 minutes to prepare myself for the onslaught of guilt and desperation. The nurse came in to check on me and brought the ice chips. I heard a commotion out in the hallway. "Sir, it's after visiting hours! You cannot just barge in here." Then I heard a thump and a slide. Danni ran past the room, stopped, did a double take on the door number and hurried in pushing the nurse out of the way.

"Oh my God! Artie, I was so worried." She threw herself on me and completely showered me with kisses. I didn't mind the pain to be honest and I am glad to know at least one of my body parts was reacting properly. Then new pain set in as I found out there was a catheter in my rapidly responding organ. Somehow through the hair, I saw the ominous outline of Claud slip in the room.

"Well, you don't look like a complete piece of shite," he quipped. He was holding one of the tablets tapping away furiously. The nurse started stammering something about visiting hours and Claud stopped his tapping to slowly meet his sunglass covered visage to her hardened stare. She looks like she could win in a scrap if it came down to it, but there was something in Claud's carriage and stance that made her falter midword. "You might want to go and check on your baby attending, Nurse Janice," as he looked at her name badge. "He practically shite his pants when he passed out."

The nurse scurried out of the way and Danni continued her osculation onslaught. It was a bit difficult for me to get a word in, but I didn't mind. There were a lot of grunts and hmms from Claud as he read the chart. "Well, looks like apart from the memory loss and sore throat from the trach tube, you are good to go home, Mr. Pax. It might take you a few days before you can hit the trail again, which I am sure Miss Zevesdochka will excuse the delay, since you were hospitalized. I will make sure you are checked out immediately." Claud left the room in search of someone to do just that. I had no doubt that he could get it done.

I heard more hurried footsteps and another clamor in the hallway. "I am his MOTHER!" I heard that wonderful matronly voice shriek out. Ma was finally here and I didn't have the power or the inclination to push Danni off. My mother burst into the room with a nurse in tow yelling about the number of unauthorized people coming to visit so late at night, Ma was about to retaliate when she saw my red haired succubus smothering me with her affections. That made her pause in her tracks.

"Arthur?" in her best worried, but suspicious, but annoyed, but hopeful voice. "Am I interrupting something or have you been worrying me for nothing? I hope you haven't gotten hitched again, without telling me. I swear, so help me, Arthur, I will make sure you are in this hospital for another week!"

Danni stood up to my right and prepared to defend my honor when I held my hand up. "Mother, meet Danni. No we aren't married. Yes we had a date, which was three days ago. I have no memory of what happened after that." The ice chips had helped the roughness of my throat and whatever cocktail was in the IV bag, helped with the head. I was still out of breath by the end of that short state of the union speech

I had partly worked out. Danni was an added twist, but I think I covered it well enough for now.

"You don't remember leaving me to go to the club?" Danni was genuinely concerned and held my hand. My mom grabbed my left hand gently because it was full of tubes and other medical accessories.

"What club?" Mom was less irritated seeing me in this state.

"Liquid Dreams, somewhere in Broad Ripple. He is helping my sisters and I find our missing sister." When she said the name of the club, which was the second time I had heard it in the span of a few minutes, something sparked in my head. I saw a purple neon sign and my heart rate spiked again, setting off more alarms. Mom and Danni jumped and let go of my hands. The nurse pushed her way to the monitor and hit a few buttons.

"Stop making him nervous. He has been through a lot over the past few days and I have been taking care of him every night. Without. Your. Help. Now, if you will excuse me I have more patients to take care of and there has already been a lot of excitement." With that the nurse turned to leave, "Mr. Pax. My name is Janice and it has been a pleasure taking care of you. I am sure your mom and girlfriend would agree."

At the same time:
"Girlfriend?" -Mom
"Yeah, we aren't.." -Me
"I like the sound of that…" -Danni
"What?" -Me
"What… You're cute in that hospital gown." -Danni
"Arthur!?!?!" -Mom
"I swear, it was one date." -Me

"Yeah, he saw me naked before the date, even, Mama Pax." -Danni

Fuck, my life just got way more interesting. Thank god for Claud walking in with the young Dr. Jones, paperwork in hand. "Mr. Pax, we are releasing you to the care of Dr. Cabiri. He seems to be more qualified to handle memory loss than I am." He nervously looked at Claud, who stood stoically looking at the young doctor. "I will have a nurse come in and get the tubes out of you. Unfortunately, we had to cut your clothing, but we have a new set of sweats that we can offer you to wear home. Would that be okay? I mean, I know someone of your status would probably be more comfortable in a suit coat," he chuckled. Everyone else in the room looked at him puzzled by his last statement.

"What is he talking about, Artie?" My mom gave a shrug with her hands lifted to the kid doctor.

"Mrs. Pax, I am sure you are aware of his celebrity status in the world of academia? His books and lectures are mind blowing!" Claud placed his hand on the excitable junior doctor. "I am sorry, Dr. Cabiri. I was getting over excited again. I do have some paperwork for you to sign, Mr. Pax. You know...Can I get your autograph?"

Did Junior just call Claud Dr. Cabiri? What the hell was going on here? I signed the paperwork and he shuffled out the door to make way for Janice to pull out the wires, tubes and other bits and pieces. I was dreading the catheter removal from down below, but it needed to be done. I looked from my mom, to Claud to Danni and said, "Do you mind?"

"Not at all.." -Danni

"I used to change your diapers, Arthur." -Mom

"Grunt" -Claud as he turned away

The nurse just chuckled and moved the sheet to find the offending tube. "You might want to sit up a bit more for this, Mr. Pax, and when I tell you you need to cough. It'll help." I followed her instructions and braced for impact. "Ok, Mr. Pax, COUGH!"

I coughed as loud as possible as she slid the plastic tube out of the hose down below. If I said it didn't hurt, I would be bold-faced lying. Or is that bald-faced? I never knew the proper term. I'll have to look it up, well after I was finished being ripped in twain from bladder to tip. Nurse Janice, pulled out the offending tube, which looked more like a crazy straw and waived it about a bit, just to watch me go queasy. The old biddie had a bit of a sadistic streak. She wrapped that and all the other bits of medical paraphernalia, nodded to my mom and as she was leaving, she looked at Danni and simply said, "He's a keeper, if you know what I mean." and mouthed O M G to her.

If I could have melted down right then and there into a puddle, I would have, just to escape. The rest of the party was chuckling at my expense and Chuck popped his head in.

"What did I miss?"

Chapter Twenty Two
Emotions and the Crave Case

On the ride home, which consisted of Claud, Danni, Ma, Chuck and myself, I had a ton of questions; about Liquid Dreams, about Dr. Claud, about the state of Danni and myself, about how Chuck got there and most importantly how I was found looking like I was in an accident or mugged with no broken bones, no major cuts and bruises and no memory about everything, but my stomach took over. I hadn't had a solid meal since the date and was feeling it. I asked Claud quietly to find the nearest White Castle, because it was the only thing that would help kickstart my appetite and lead to better food. I know that you non-natives have probably seen that movie about two stoners going on a drug fueled adventure to find the perfect stoner food. It's pretty good and has Doogie Howser in it. One of the leads talks about finding that perfect food to satisfy that itch in their stomach that could only be satisfied by those perfectly steamed square burgers. Yeah it was like that for me, too. I had been through hell and back and needed something normal.

The rest of the car was questioning my sanity and Claud simply said, "He is my patient, now and has been through a great ordeal. If he needs some kind of normalcy in his life, God Dammit, he's going to get some. Do any of you lot have an objection?" God Dammit, Claud was growing on me.

"So, are we going to discuss this 'doctor' thing or is it just going to be one of those unspoken oddities about you?" I was genuinely concerned he had committed a felony by impersonating a medical professional.

Claud smiled at me and simply said, "All in good time, Mr. Pax. All in good time."

Food ordered, we headed back to my house through the falling snow. Chuck took possession of the food bags, Danni held the drinks and Mom held herself together. It wasn't a snowmageddon, like it had been a few days ago, but it was still pretty heavy. The road crews were working on the main roads everywhere just to stay on top of it. The car was full of happy conversations as the passengers got to know each other. It was nice having all the people I care about in one place. Even Claud.

It didn't take us long to get to my house. Traffic was non-existent and it seemed every stoplight behaved for us and let us slide through with very few stops. As we pulled up, mom's eyes got a bit misty when she saw her former house. All the memories of me growing up came rushing back.

A great wracking sob escaped from her chest. "I could have lost you and never known, Artie. I felt like the worst mother on the planet that we couldn't find you. I was hoping that you were just off on another lecture that you forgot to tell me about at first. Then, when Charles called me. I lost it. I am sorry for jumping down your throat at the hospital. I was distraught and my imagination got the better of me."

My mom was never one to break down like this in public. I know it was in a car, but there were two people in the car she had just met tonight. And she never cried around anyone, let alone me. I did my best to comfort her as Claud got out to let out the contents of his passenger area. He walked up to the door and unlocked it, went in and started turning on lights, to everyone else's surprise.

"Um, I kind of have a roommate for a bit." I admitted sheepishly. We all climbed out and Claud magically appeared at my side to help me up the path and steps to the door. It was cozy inside and sounded like the kettle was on already. Claud got me sitting on the couch and Danni handed me my drink and followed Chuck into the kitchen to get plates and divvy up our late night craving feast. Claud poured himself and Mom some tea and delivered them on a silver serving tray I didn't know I had.

Mom teared up again. "This was your grandparents' set. They got it on their honeymoon in France. Shirley and I always played tea and fought over who would get it after they died. Little did we know they would be taken from us at such a young age. She doesn't know that I hid it." She let out a sob and tried to disguise it as a laugh. Mom really knows how to bring a mood down, but she usually had a reason for bringing things up like this. "I had always hoped to give it to my grandkids for them to play tea with."

And there it was the "I don't have grandkids" speech. I really wasn't in the mood for it, so I tried to just ignore her and eat my sliders. Thankfully, Claud asked for some help in the kitchen and they left. Danni looked a bit embarrassed and Chuck was trying very hard to not bust out laughing. I finished my soda and let out a loud belch, now it was my turn to look embarrassed. I looked between Danni and Chuck and they burst out in laughter. I couldn't help but laugh too. It hurt, but dammit it was the stress relief I needed.

After our fit of joy for me being alive, I yawned so big I practically unhinged my jaw. Danni looked at me with such caring and love in her eyes. "Come on hero, let's get you to bed." She stood up and held out a hand, which I gladly took and followed her to my bedroom. She started undressing me to get me in bed. She was caring and very gentle as she helped me lay down.

"I can't sleep until you tell me everything that happened after the date. I assume you came with me to this mystery club?" Even though I was exhausted I needed answers.

"I didn't. I had to go home and tend to the stables, which is where I should be right now, but you are more important to my family." She smiled shyly.

"What about you? Am I important to you?" Man, I can't believe I just said that. I blame the drugs and sliders for my new found confidence.

Danni leaned in and did the motion for me to scoot over. "You are very important to me, Artie. I can take the night off tonight, if you want me to? I didn't like the feeling of losing you. I know it's crazy since we have only known each other for a short time but I think I am falling for you."

My mind reeled and all I could do was reach out to pull her in for a snuggle hug. I kissed her forehead. She looked up into my eyes and softly kissed my lips. "I should go call Rochelle and update her. I can also have Claud drive everyone else home, if you'd like?"

"A night in your arms would help heal me faster than any miracle drug on the market." We kissed again and she peeled out of the bed with that grace I saw her use on our first meeting. A few minutes of quiet conversation and Claud came in my room with a cup of water, a few pills and a glass of something that looked medicinal. "So, 'Doctor', do you have anything to comment on this development?"

Claud smiled and handed me the water and pills which I took dutifully. "Well, maybe I wasn't exactly truthful about my position in the Army and my life leading up to it. I went to medical school to study internal medicine and when Desert Storm was started by your president, I felt compelled to join the fight. I am a man of many hidden talents, Mr. Pax. Such as this one." He handed me the dark colored liquid.

"Dare I ask what it is Dr. Hidden Talents?" He just smiled at me and shook his head.

"It'll help, trust me." He waited for me to drain the liquid. It was kind of sweet and earthy. I started to feel better already. Claud collected the empty glass and pill container. He left the water on my nightstand. "I will be back after taking your mother and friend home. Ms. Danni will be your nursemaid for the interim. And dare I say, sir, I've never seen her take a shining to anyone as much as you. Treat her well. She is a very special lady."

Great, now he's dispensing relationship advice as well as medicine. He turned and left as Danni made her way back in putting her phone in the back pocket of her jeans. She waited until Mom and Chuck had come into my room to say goodbye. They all left and it was just me and Danni. The delightful Danni. The Danni who was removing her clothes. The quickly nude Danni. I was suddenly glad the catheter was not invading my privacy. She stopped at the side of the bed and coyly looked at me. "Is this alright? I don't like sleeping with clothes on. It's too restricting." All I could do was smile and pull back the sheets.

Chapter Twenty Three
Memories

I know I am dreaming, mostly because I have seen it all before. The pond, the mist, the predawn sun, the figure standing to keep them at bay. This time I was able to move my legs. I walked calmly over to the shadowy figure as the spirits started to climb over the banks. The figure started to spin the red ray and work his magic.

As I walked steadily toward my scarlet savior, The light became bright enough to see features defining his face. A grey beard spilled over his dark robes. His cowl was less of a hood and more like the headdress of the Russian Old Believers, a rounded stiff skull cap with black cloth draped down the back. Red Cyrillic symbols with geometric shapes adorned the black robes that seemed to shine with the same light from the death ray.

I walked up to his side as the ray burst forth and destroyed the spirits. He didn't look away from his prey until they were all gone or back into the pond. He then turned to me and said something in Russian. I had no clue what he said to me. I tried to tell him as much, but he continued with his lecture. He became more passionate and animated. As the daylight grew, I saw his robes weren't covered in red embroidery thread, but silver. Pure silver that twisted and turned like strands of cotton.

He took a deep breath in and loudly yelled, "Protect the egg!" in clear English.

He continued speaking in Russian and when he finished speaking, he turned away to walk toward a simple oval hut near the treeline that had a stable next to it. Another figure pulled up on a chariot that had wheels which shone like the full moon. He stepped off to greet the aged monk. I couldn't see much of him, other than the standard Old Believer's robes with gilded runes covering it, was a long white beard. They embraced and the gilded monk went into the hut, whereas the silver-gilt monk walked to the stable, where a familiar red-head stood with his chariot. His chariot blazed red and yellow like the rising sun and was very difficult to look at.

The wheel grew in brightness and intensity until I had to cover my eyes. When it was dark enough to uncover my eyes I was standing in front of the club Liquid Dreams and everything about that night came flooding back.

I tried to sit up in bed with the sudden realization of what happened to make me miss three days, only to be pulled back down by the surprisingly strong arms of my bunk mate. I had nearly forgotten that Danni was lying next to me in nothing but what God had given her. So, I lay there rehashing everything that had happened that night. The creepy ticket booth attendant, the coat check girl, the orgie, the owner, the drink and smoke and finally Allie, er, Rusalka. The rest of the night was snippets of what had happened.

The owner saying something about having mortals dance was such a joy to watch and rather invigorating. A couple of mortals leading me out to the dance floor. I was compelled to dance while the music was on. There were breaks for drinking and restroom, but while the music was on we all danced. I remember being led to a door and stairs that went down. Then another door with beds strewn about. Only to rise again to dance upstairs.

By the next morning, I realized what was going on and tried to break out of the spell I was under. I was able to break free and find Rusalka. Guards heard the ruckus, because she was adamant about leaving. They grabbed me, roughed me up, made me drink something that tasted foul and you know the rest. This memory flash made my mind reel. I was upset with myself for rushing into a situation that I had no idea what the dangers were. Felix would have been pissed with me. He always stressed the importance of being prepared.

I lay there in my reverie about the past noticing that Danni's breathing was steady and even. Even sleeping, with her hair all askew, she was still stunning. The next thing I noticed was the aches and pains I felt earlier were completely gone. Whatever Claud had given me had worked its magic. The final thing I noticed was Danni was as heavy as a dead elephant and wasn't budging, so I relaxed back down under her and drifted back to sleep with the idea of what to research and which potions to craft. I had a pretty good idea what I was dealing with, so I needed to prepare. In a few days, I was going clubbing again.

Chapter Twenty Four
War, Hooh, Good Gawd
November 21

I woke the next morning and Danni had already risen. I smelled the tantalizing aroma of *shbyten* coming from the kitchen. I rose, feeling invigorated and ready to tackle my notes and the internet. Claud must have heard me stir with his super hearing, the blind bastard, because I heard him rise up and start cooking. A few mumbled words passed between my two house guests and the soft footsteps of the smaller of the two came padding into the bedroom again.

"Good morning, handsome." Danni purred. "How are you feeling?" She put on a pouty face and I realized she was wearing one of my house robes. I kept a few around just in case someone crashes in the library. Some were lighter for summer. She was wearing one of the lighter ones that clung to her chilly body.

I gulped and she giggled. "Oh, I see that you are already rising." Danni walked to the side of the bed she was sleeping on, lifted the sheets and she pouted her lips. "Too bad. I guess I will have to come back later. I was hoping to help you get up." She turned to leave and I grabbed her hand.

"You are not going anywhere, Nurse Danni." I pulled her into bed with me. Surprisingly, I felt like a new man. Then came the kissing and the nibbling and well… other things. We revelled in our new found status, whatever that was exactly until a knock came on the partly open door.

"I truly am sorry, but breakfast is served." Claud beat a quick retreat to the kitchen and started plating up the Full Breakfast he crafted once again. Danni pulled back and her stomach grumbled loud enough for the neighbors to hear.

"I am famished. I guess we will have to do this again later?" She nibbled on my earlobe and I sighed. I have not been this turned on since Ex-Zilla and honestly it kind of scared me. We rose without another word and dressed enough to not be indecent. It was a lovely morning. The sun was shining, the ravens were croaking, the food looked and smelled divine and we tucked in. In between bites, I filled them both in on the memories that had invaded my dreams. Claud and Danni listened with rapt attention.

"So what do you think we are dealing with?" Claud asked.

"I am almost certain, it is the Fae. I have to do some checking with my contacts as to who are the leaders of the kingdom here, but that shouldn't take too long. For now, let's do nothing. We need a good plan of attack and to know exactly what we are up against." Danni and Claud sullenly nodded their heads. We finished our meal and Claud rose to start cleaning up.

Danni took my hand and pulled it to her lips. "Is there anything I can do to help?" I sighed and shrugged my shoulders. "Do you have an extra laptop? I have a few things I can check out as well. I have some people I can message. You know, being alive for quite a while, I've accumulated a few trustworthy contacts." She winked at me. It kind of shook me a bit realizing that even though she looked younger than me, she was much, much older and I was okay with that. It wasn't just the sex like it had been with Char. There was something much deeper between us and I wanted to explore that, after I liberated her sister and the rest of the entrapped people.

I nodded and we both rose and went into the study. I booted up my system, then booted up the laptop I use for lectures and we both got to work. Time passed quickly throughout the day and Claud made sure we had plenty of food and caffeine to keep us going. There were little breaks for quick smooches with Danni and I realized I've never had a partner that could keep up with me while working. I mean, I'm not very needy, but every once in a while I just like to take small romance breaks. My other girlfriends and ex hated that I got so wrapped up in research mode and eventually ended up ignoring them. I didn't feel that way at all with Danni.

She was just as engrossed looking things up and every time I looked at her, she was biting her lower lip in concentration while reading things online waiting for her contacts to message back, or looking at me with mutual admiration.

I wanted to bring up the rest of the dream, but I didn't feel like the time was right since we were on a deadline. By dinner time, I had a solid outline of a plan. I had to call in a few favors with my police contacts to get some information, but I promised them to be kept in the loop about when and where it was all going down, because they could alert EMTs and the Fire Rescue to come and help triage all the captives. I have worked with a few officers in the past on other oddity cases and have earned their and their captain's trust.

I called a war room meeting in the kitchen.

"Okay, what we have here is a case of a rogue Fae that has started glamouring and feeding on mortals. I don't know how they were able to sway Allie, nor keep her under their thrall. I was able to break out fairly easily, but whatever roofie they slipped me to get me out of there, was a doozy. I kind of need to find someone on the inside to get more intel, but we just don't have time for that. I want to get this wrapped up in a few days." I then went on to detail my thoughts. Claud added and subtracted from places that wouldn't work. He had also made a few calls, so we wouldn't be going in without backup. He also said he had supplies for us to use; earpieces for communication, tracking watches and all kinds of other special forces doohickies, it's a technical term.

The plan would take place tomorrow morning at the earliest.

Chapter Twenty Five

Faentervention

Danni had to go back home to tend to her duties in the stable. I would have loved to have spent another night with her, but there was a lot of planning to do and not a lot of time. First thing's first, I had to go visit the local Duchy.

The Fae have a society of their own amongst normal society. It is the perfect case of humans and nonhumans living right next to each other, but humans not paying attention. The ruling class of the Fae, the Tuatha de Danann, started in Ireland. There have been Fae around the globe living in their own little pockets and glades and most humans ignored them. Every clan had their own leaders and rules, until the Scientific Revolution.

The mid 1500s were a tumultuous time for humans and Fae. After Martin Luther nailed his "the pope is bad and here is why" statement he named Ninety-five Theses or Disputation on the Power of Indulgences, the Fae communities had started to come out of the glades and nature pockets to try and integrate into human culture. It was going great until the Scientific Revolution started in 1543 CE. When the world started to become less mystical and more ordered, it drove the Fae nuts. They loved the attention humans were giving them, even if the humans didn't even know they were paying fealty to a Faerie overlord. It further made it more difficult for the Fae to live in cities several centuries later when the Industrial Revolution came to be.

Hundreds and thousands of Fae were killed just due to iron factories and the fallout from the ashes they created. So the Fae either had to withdraw to the deep forests, find some hidden dimensional pocket or die. And many did. Entire civilizations of Fae were wiped out. Many of their secrets and hidden knowledge were forever lost. The tribes started to band together and help the human peasants lead revolutions of their own. From the mid-1700s up to the early 1900s, Irish Tuatha de Danann were leading every peasant led revolution from behind the scenes. Sabotage, crops burning, even the assassination of several world leaders were all the machinations of the Fae pulling the heart strings of humans.

While the Tuatha de Danann were leading the revolutions, they also started building an empire, one that rivaled any of the world powers, only in secret. Ireland became their seat of power and they started carving up Europe into smaller sections. After all of the country lines were established in the governments of humanity, the Fae also established their own seat of power. The titles are the same as in the English Peerage titles. In America, There is one Duke and Duchess for the continent, three Marquees for each country, in each country there is an earl for each time zone, so the US has four, and finally in each time zone, there is a viscount for each state. All of this was looked over by a benevolent King Oberon and Queen Titania. It gets a bit confusing.

I have no idea where the owner of the club lay in the grand scheme of things, but one of my contacts keeps up with the Tuatha's bloodlines and where they currently are. It just so happens that the Duke and Duchess of our sector were visiting the viscount of Indiana. They were cousins and apparently they stayed in close contact with each other. Which was great for me. With the address in hand, I grabbed my coat and walked out the door. Claud had already started the car and was waiting to open my door. I handed him the slip of paper and we were off.

I knew I had enough time to review customs and court etiquette. The local Viscount and his consort were Count Edgar and Lady Shariah de Gwent. They moved in a few years ago after the old Viscounts had retired. Contrary to popular belief, the Fae are not immortal, they just have longer lifespans than humans. In the older times, they would just move to another part of the world to avoid humans from finding out they weren't aging. Now it was customary that the offices were switched out every sixty years or so.

They still had problems with conspiracy theorists and photos showing up on the internet. They handle them as best as they can. There is a theory that Keanu Reeves is an immortal. He's just Fae and doesn't want anything to do with court life.

The Duke Liam and Duchess Siobhan de Sligo have been in charge of North America for the past fifty years and are due to retire soon. They lived in Newfoundland for the majority of the year and did an annual pilgrimage to each of their favorite cousins around the holidays. De Sligo was of the Unseelie court and his powers were strongest in the winter months, so he didn't fear attack around the holidays. There was a lot of courtly intreague and murder attempts, but most of those were kept inhouse.

We pulled up to a rather swanky looking house. Oddly enough, there was no gate, so we pulled up in the circular driveway and Claud parked near the front door. He did his chauffeur duties and went up to ring the doorbell. It opened and he did his formal announcement of me. I guess it went well, because he quickly came back and opened the car door. We were ushered inside and our coats were gently removed. We were led into a large parlour with four people already seated around a roaring fire. They were dressed comfortably, but obviously did not shop at the local Target.

The older gentleman stood and extended his hand. His hair was salt and pepper, and he looked about as Irish as you can. "Mr. Pax! What an unusual pleasure it is to meet you! I am Viscount Edgar de Gwynt. This is my lovely wife, Shariah," he indicated a dark skinned beauty that looked ageless, except for the first beginnings of white hair on her temples. Her hair was pulled back into a simple bun. It wasn't surprising for me to see a biracial couple, because it was Indianapolis, but I was surprised to hear a light Irish accent come from her lips as she greeted me.

The Viscount waved his hand toward the other couple seated and introduced the Duke and Duchess, to which I bowed. They looked like a lighthouse keeper and his wife. Not at all what I was expecting. I was ushered to a seat and asked if I wanted anything to drink. My fear kicked in because the last time I had a drink in the presence of the Fae... well you know.

The Duke smiled at me, "Don't worry Mr. Pax, it isn't laced with anything, just regular cognac that we brought from Canada." His Newfey accent was delightful. I graciously accepted. It's not every day you get Newfoundland cognac from a Duke.

"To what do we owe this pleasure, Mr. Pax?" asked the Duchess.

"I feel like I am at a disadvantage here. You all seem to know about me, but I do not know much about any of you." I was being as perfectly fucking genteel as possible. The cognac was wonderfully smoky and sweet.

The Viscountess smiled, "We all know about your work and admire how you speak for all the non mortals that inhabit the world. Yes, you use the guise of mythology as your basis, but we appreciate everything you have done for all races of 'monsters' as the world calls us."

"Your accolades are high praise. Thank you, Viscountess." We all took sips of our libations. "I don't want to come off as presumptuous or rude on our first meeting, but something has happened here in town and I thought you should know about it, before I took matters into my own hands." They exchanged looks of confusion. "A new club has opened. It is Fae run, which is perfectly fine, but I was hired to find a missing person. A demigoddess to be precise. For some reason she is being held against her wishes, which shouldn't be possible. I know this because the owner tried to ensorcell me as well."

The Viscount looked distressed. "I am assuming you are talking about Liquid Dreams. The owner, Wellington Forbes, has a legitimate business license in both in accordance with mortal and Fae law. I was just there the other night checking out the legitimacy of his operation. It is not common knowledge that us Fae need to have mortal energy to sustain us when it is not our season. Most of the patrons this time of the year are of the Seelie court. You see, there is nothing untoward going on."

"Begging your pardon, your Lordship, but there is something untoward going on there. I was drugged, made to dance all night and then led to an underground cell to sleep along with all the workers and other dancers. I was able to break out of the spell due to my training. I found my charge and was accosted, beaten up, drugged again and hospitalized for three days." I tried to keep my voice under control, but it was difficult to. I looked at the Fae courtiers and their faces were unreadable. "I am coming to you as a formality to let you know, I fully intend to rescue at least the person I was hired to find, because it is vitally important she is able to do her duties when her time comes." I placed the unfinished drink on an end table, ignoring the coaster on purpose and stood to leave.

The Duke had a meaningful glance with the Viscount but no one said anything to stop me. "I hope that this meeting doesn't leave a foul taste in your mouth. I would like to be allowed to have further, more academic discussion with you."

I turned to walk out of the room. "Mr. Pax, I know you will do what you must for your charge. I will tell you this, though. If any of my subjects are harmed, a second meeting will be less than pleasant. The only reason you are not being dealt with right now, is you are protected as a guest. We Fae treat our guests very well. We treat our enemies quite the opposite. I hope we can remain friendly." With that they all rose and walked out of the room, clearly dismissing me.

Chapter Twenty Six

While I was drinking with the Duchy, Claud's strike team was checking out the club. Inside and out they took notes on entrances, exits, air ducts, fire escapes and possible windows. They had a detailed report ready for us when we met back at the house. The plan was to infiltrate just before the sun rose and liberate Allie before the guards knew any better. I didn't need the highest ranking Fae in this hemisphere to be upset with me.

We went over the plan several times and then packed it in for the night. Claud's crew was very tight knit as if they had been working together for a very long time. Not much was said between them, they absorbed the data and nodded a lot as Claud and I gave our intel.

Claud's team consisted of five members; he just called them the Dactyls. They each had a number one through five, but in Greek; Ena, Dio, Tria, Tessera and Pente. They all looked similar in shape, size and appearance, it was as if they were clones of each other. Their personalities were far from identical.

Ena was by far the leader of the group. He was of few words, but had his team so well trained that all he had to do was point and the rest knew what he wanted them to do. Dio was very flippant and sarcastic in his remarks, he was the team sharpshooter. Tria seemed to be the playboy of the group. In the short span of me meeting him, he had lined up at least four dates after the excursion tonight. He was the communications expert, he knew how to hack into most electronics to monitor comms. Tessera seemed to be the drinker in the group, he was a functioning alcoholic with a slight pink hue to his cheeks, but one damn good brawler. Finally, rounding out the team was Penta. He was a bit more stocky than the rest, but a damn good explosives expert and lockpick.

It was a fitful sleep for me that night, but I knew I needed to be ready to go and rested. I don't remember dreaming, which I usually do, but there was a certain level of stress that kept me out of a full REM sleep.

There was no breakfast prepped that morning, but there was a pot of stiff black coffee and with the nervous energy I had stored up, that was all I needed. I had righteous indignation on my side, and the need for justice for the trapped mortals and Allie.

As far as plans went, this was fairly simple. We were going to break in the back door, which was Penta's speciality. If there were guards that gave us any trouble I had a few potions ready to knock the guards out and a few nonlethal spells at the ready. Claud, Tria and Tessera were going to be the muscle that would wrestle down anyone that needed wrestling. Dio was going to cover our backs and Ena would be lookout to sweep the area. We were ready to go, so we went.

Their large, nondescript, white van with no windows slid silently through the snow. Morning commuters had just started to join together for work and some grocery shopping for the upcoming feast holiday. We pulled in the alley behind the club and set to work.

Ena immediately grabbed the fire escape ladder and climbed up top to be a lookout. Penta took out his tools and made short work of the lock. He then slid in a flying drone to check out the backstage area, which was clear. The rest of us slipped in and silently shut the door. I led the team to the basement door with no complications. This next part was the part that could get hairy. Penta and Dio stayed in the backstage area to help cover our escape if it came to that.

Down the steps, we went to Allie's "dressing room" which was unguarded. Claud opened the door and scanned the interior. He motioned us inside, however our thugs stayed out to make sure no one snuck up from behind. We found her sleeping on a four post bed on the far side of a large vanity. She looked very pale in the dim light. We crept closer to the bed.

Then the overhead light came on. Claud and I turned to see the door slam shut and lock. Wellington Forbes stood next to the door and clapped his hands. "Congratulations, Mr. Pax. You got back into my stronghold. Good for you." His smile doubled. "Now, I believe you are trespassing and I will have to deal with you directly."

He flicked his wrist towards me and I flew up against the wall which rung my bell pretty hard. Claud pulled out a throwing knife from somewhere and threw it at Forbes, who deflected it easily. I shook my head and since I was still within reach of my assailant, I reached to pull Forbes' legs out from under him. Literally. I grabbed his pants and pulled. He went down in a swearing heap. The door started rattling as the rest of the team was trying to break in to help, but it held fast.

Forbes spun out a few tendrils of power to wrap myself and Claud up in invisible bands. We were stuck fast like prey in a spider's web. He raised himself from the ground and dusted himself off.

"Did you really think this would be easy, Mr. Pax?" he chuckled as the door kept rattling. "I knew you were going to be coming back to liberate Rusalka. Yes, I knew who she was from the moment I sent out the email to her. She has become a vital part of my organization to lure in mortals. We needed them to be able to feed and be able to grow more powerful. For you see, if Rusalka isn't there to herald in the spring rains, it will be time for the Unseelie to reign forever in a neverending winter. I just didn't take into consideration your strength in the mystical arts. I will not make the same mistake."

"Forbes, I love that you are doing the whole expositional villain speech, but really, do you have to do it so over dramatically?" I was working to loosen the bands around my arms. "I had already figured out the majority of your plot. The only thing I don't understand is, how did you get the Mahaha to attack me? I know he is basically an Unseelie Fae, but he doesn't come this far south. It's too warm for him."

Forbes had a shocked look on his face. "Mahaha? I have nothing to do with that psychopath. He gets his jollies off by flaying his victims alive. I have never killed any of my charges. Well, not intentionally. It's not my fault that mortals cannot dance like they used to. No, this adds a new wrinkle to our plans."

"*Our* plans?" I was perplexed by his admission. I was certain he had sent the Mahaha to throw us off the trail. "I mean since we are your prisoner, you might as well spill, Forbes. We aren't going anywhere." Oh, but we were. I had almost been able to get one hand out to get a potion vial that had a sleeping potion which affects Fae and not humans. I hope I used the right herbs.

"No, Mr. Pax. It will not be that easy to get the information you so deeply desire. Just know that there are much grander schemes in the works than just keeping you and Rusalka here forever. I have taken a particular liking to her dance style and hope I can keep her around for a very long time as my concubine." At that, she finally opened her eyes and shakily sat up.

"You will never have me." she said weakly. Her eyes were full of tears and I could tell she was being kept against her wishes, unlike a few days ago. It seemed his grip was loosening on her. Forbes made his way to her bed and stroked her cheek with one of his manicured hands.

"Oh, my darling, I already do. You just don't know it, yet." She tried to pull back from his hand, but couldn't move. Then, three things happened at the same time. I was able to loosen my hand and pull out the stopper from the small beaker. The door burst open with the two brute paratroopers. And a vent from overhead burst open as the rooftop watch came rappelling in. The inside guards were tussling with two very large looking Fae guards.

Forbes grabbed Rusalka's neck and held a dagger to it. It came from one of his fingernails, and slowly it grew in length and sharpness. Allie cried out. Claud struggled against his bands and finally broke free. Everyone had everyone else covered. It was a typical Old West standoff. No one moved.

"One move and she dies, Mr. Pax." Forbes snarled. His calm demeanor had been replaced with a wilder, more unkempt look. Allie sobbed and everyone else just held their breath. That's when the whole building shook with a sound that could only be explained as a roaring bleat, as if an unholy union of a tiger and a goat had stepped into the playing field.

"Ah, I see that another uninvited guest has arrived, just in time to make our escape," Forbes took a step towards the wall with the vanity, with Allie still in his clutches. The bleating roar sounded again and it was accompanied with a couple of shouts, a gunshot and a muffled explosion. Which redoubled the roar, followed by the sound of two thuds on the floor above us.

Tria went to the stairs to see what was going on. The ominous sounds of large steps thudded across the backstage area to the stairwell accentuated by the tinkling of chains. Tria yelled out and was silenced just as fast accompanied by a deafening bleat-roar, another loud thud and Tria's body sailing back to land at Tessera's feet.

The room became overwhelmed with the smell of wet dog, rusted iron and the pungent eau de parfum of goat. The smell was so overwhelming Tessera, Ena, Claud and myself were gagging. I held my hand up to my nose to try and diffuse the cloying odor, but to no avail. It was already in my nose and subsequently in my tastebuds.

I scanned the room quickly only to see Forbes and Allie in the full length mirror next to the vanity. Not in front, but actually in the mirror, what I didn't see was the rest of the occupants of the room being reflected. Fucking fae magic. Another bellow brought my attention to our new assailant.

It hulked out filling the door frame. The twisted horns on its head scraped the jamb and it had to twist its head to fit them inside. A full goat head with blood shot golden hourglass shaped eyes peered at each of us from under its furrowed brow. The klip klop of its cloven hooves were the source of the thudding from upstairs and in its taloned hands were a large wooden switch and a cloth sack. The two most frightening parts of this Austrian horror were the lengthy chains that were draped over its shoulders and its mouth, which split into a Cheshire grin that proudly showed its stained fangs. A head taller than Claud, the creature was something out of my nightmares, like literally. I had dreamed of this exact thing as a child, oddly enough it was usually in December, I thrashed about in my bed worrying that it would come and steal me away as it did one of my childhood friends.

I was so struck with fear, I could only whimper its name, "Krampus."

Chapter Twenty Seven
Interlude: I Don't want to Krampus Your Style

When thinking about the end of the year holidays, many people immediately think about the mythical figure who dons a red velvet suit, trimmed in white fur to stave off the arctic winds of the North Pole, Santa Claus. His cheery disposition as the corpulent patron saint of good will and holiday wishes have been floating around in the collective minds of people around the world for centuries. Santa and his elves deliver toys to the good children who believe in him on the evening of Christmas. This brings happy thoughts to many people. What these people don't know is there are many "anti-Santas" that haunt the nightmares of children around the globe as well.

Many of these tales have been pushed to the wayside due to oral traditions not being kept up with in this modern age of high definition and faster than light transmissions via computer, cell phone and electronic tablet. Tales like Frau Perchta, Belsnickel, Black Peter, and Gryla are still tame in comparison to the Alpine belief in Krampus.

There is no exact origin to the stories of Krampus, but all of the tales agree that Krampus is the counterpart of Saint Nicholas. Where St. Nicholas is jolly and delivers gifts of fruit, nuts and small toys on December the 6th, Krampus scours the countryside looking for naughty children the night before. The evil goat man hybrid went from village to village looking for naughty children to punish. Covered in dark fur, cloven hooves, a tail and great curved horns adorning his head, Krampus has many characteristics that also adorn the ideas of the Christian Devil. The one thing that separates Krampus from the Devil is his tongue, which is great and snakelike and can always be seen lolling outside of his fanged mouth.

Krampus always had chains and bells wrapped around himself, a basket strapped to his back, a birch switch in his hand and a sack in his other hand. On the evening of Krampusnacht, which is December the 5th, he would weigh the misdeeds of the children. If they were found naughty, he would use his switch to lash them. If the children were downright evil, he would chain them up, stuff them in his basket and take them to Hell for an entire year to torutre out the bad. If the children were beyond reform, Krampus would simply feast on them, alive. Now, if a child repented of their misdeeds, he would let them go with a stern warning. Sometimes, the children would place the blame on another child for their naughtiness. If the child that the finger was pointed at was guilty, into the sack they went. If the child was good and falsely accused, a bell would be given to them off of Krampus' chain and be spared.

Of late, celebrating Kranpusnacht has become widely popular in the United States but it has been an ongoing tradition in the Alps. Europeans started sending Krampuskarten, Krampus greeting cards, to each other in the 1800s. And depending on where you are, you might even be treated to an annual parade of people clad in Krampus outfits called a Krampuslauf. The annual Krampuslauf are becoming more popular in the Americas, specifically, the United States and Canada.

As a child I had a friend of mine, named Jonathan, disappear in the early part of December. We all thought he ran away because of his alcoholic and abusive father, what we didn't know at the time was he was a very naughty boy and was taken away by Krampus. He came back home in early January, clothes all in tatters, but holding a bell. One of those you might see on a reindeer harness, not a ringing bell like on a shop door. However, these bells were forged in the heat of a dying volcano and sounded like ice cracking on Lake Baikal in the spring. If you held one of these bells up to the moon, you would see the secret runes that were written on them. The writing was so fine, that only the pure of heart could read the message without magnification.

I know all of this because when Jonathan came back he handed me the bell for safe keeping. I still keep that bell on me at all times, just in case. I do not know what happened to him, because after he returned the police came to take statements from all of the parents in the neighborhood and were asking questions about Jonathan's father. The night of his return, his mother took him to the hospital to get him examined and they found multiple lash marks on his backside both old and new. His father was arrested and he and his mother moved away before the new year. That was the last I saw of Jonathan. However, I do remember seeing cloven hoof prints in the neighborhood and at first thought it was from reindeer, not that they were popular in Indianapolis, but it was close to Christmas. I just didn't take into consideration how deep the prints were in the snow, nor that there were only two instead of four.

And this was just the beginning of children disappearing over a ten year period. It was never more than ten at a time, but every year there was a rash of kids missing around the beginning of December. The police were confused but after a decade, the disappearances just stopped. In the years that we had snow, the strange footprints were seen around the houses, but because they were not boot trod prints and looked closer to deer prints, the police thought nothing of it.

However, us children started seeing and hearing things that made our boots shake. The horrible bleating roar, the chains clanking and the glimpses of the giant horned upright goat that we all came to know as Krampus haunted our dreams.

There were rumors of a small group of friends that went after Krampus to stop his reign of terror, but those were largely unsubstantiated because everyone "knew someone who knew someone that was friend's with one of the four kids" but no one knew them directly. I guess it will be a mystery until someone Scooby Doo's it out.

However, back to the present.

Chapter Twenty Eight
The Final Countdown

The five of us stood looking at each other. Krampus in the doorway shifted his massive bulk, Claud, Tessera, and Ena all took a slight step back. I was firmly rooted in place. Then Krampus did something unexpected. He started singing. In a deep baritone that rumbled from his massive chest, he sang:

"You better not shout,
You better not cry
You better not weep
For you're going to die..."

Tessera smiled and sang back, "Santa Claus is coming to town!!!" Which made Krampus bellow again, drop his sack and charge at Tessera. His bulk belied his agility and Krampus quickly made the distance between them much shorter. However, Tessera was faster and able to sidestep like a matador. He got a couple of quick jabs on Krampus' side as he ran past. While this was happening, Ena pulled out a pistol from a concealed holster, Claud shifted his feet subtly to be in a ready to fight stance and I stood there rooted in place with my mouth slightly agape.

A quick shot fired from Ena's pistol at close range caused Krampus to turn and whip out his chains toward the source of the sound. The thick chain disarmed Ena almost completely. Ena's arm was knocked out of socket as Krampus smiled again and said "Naughty," as he swiped out with the burch switch in his other hand. I have no idea what kind of wood it was, but even though it looked like a loose collection of sticks, it was strong as steel and ripped through Ena's protective vest deep into his chest. Ena fell clutching his wounds.

Tessera stepped up again to throw a few more punches before trying to get to Ena and Krampus swiped out with his claws. Tessera never had a chance. He also collapsed in a heap bleeding from the multiple wounds in his torso area. Then Krampus turned on me as if dismissing Claud.

He cocked his head to the side and sniffed the air as if he was smelling the fear oozing out of my pores like a cheap cologne. Claud took the initiative at the momentary distraction and stepped in to get a kidney shot. Krampus reached out and grabbed Claud by the face and threw him against the wall without even looking. My heart was racing. I was really and truly fucked. Krampus had taken out an entire team of highly trained professional, um, whatever they were. I had no chance.

Krampus sniffed the air again. "I know you, boy," he rumbled. "I have tasted your fear before. A sweet intoxicating smell that I can't exactly put my finger on. What is your name?"

I tried to open my mouth, but it stayed shut.

"Oh, the strong silent type," he chuckled again, which was closer to a Clausian ho-ho-ho than the typical evil monster laugh. Not that I have heard many evil monsters laugh.

"Don't tell me, let me guess." *sniff*
"Hmm, you are a local boy" *sniff and a step towards me*

"I remember you from thirty years ago. You weren't one of the little brats that tracked me down and locked me away." Well, that confirmed that. *sniff*

"No, you are one of the ones that got away. Now, how did you do that?" *sniff and a snort this time as if he smelled something distasteful*

"Jonathan? No, I remember him, he was quite fun to, heh heh heh, reform." That chuckle sent more shivers down my spine. I could only imagine the amounts of torture my childhood friend went through all those years ago.

"If you are not Jonathan, why do you smell like him?" He took another step towards me and shoved the bed in my direction. It clattered along the floor and roughly pinned my legs against the wall trapping me. I might have lost all bladder control at that point, I'm not exactly sure.

The nightmare goat walked calmly to the bed and sat down on it making it groan under his bulk of muscles. He turned to face me and started brushing me lightly with the birch switch, which felt like tiny razor blades. He leaned forward and opened his mouth unleashing his great lolling tongue, which was the size of a cow tongue. Drool came slipping off his great worm-like tongue. His hot breath forced its way into my nose and rotted there. It was like the scene from Aliens when the queen opened her mouth at Ripley and then opened its smaller mouth, but way more squishy and a frighteningly much larger amount of spittle.

His eye focused on my neck and used a talon to pull out from under my clothes a chain that I always wore. It was a charm necklace I always wore when I went out on jobs. On this were various religious symbols, an iron horseshoe nail and the bell that Jonathan gave me. I usually kept it all tightly bound in leather to not make any noise.

Krampus looked at the necklace and back at me. "How did you get this bell?" he snarled at me.

I took a deep breath and stammered out something like "It was a gift."

Krampus once again bleat/roared right in my face and tried to rip the necklace off my person. Somehow, it stayed fast. He tried to pull it a couple more times and although he was pulling with all his strength, it not only stayed on my neck, but the necklace also didn't bite into my skin. The only thing he managed to do was rip off the leather covering around the bell. Then all hell broke loose.

The runes on the bell flared out a blinding white light that seemed to only affect Krampus. He covered his eyes and started howling as if in pain. As he let go of the necklace, a single tinkle pealed out of the bell like the ring of a great church bell that could be heard for miles away. The sound drove Krampus to his feet, off the bed.

Moving his hands from his eyes to his ears, I saw that his golden eyes were now smoking holes on the sides of his massive head, which for some reason looked smaller and less frightening. Another tintinnabulation from my necklace sounded and Krampus ripped his ears off. I mean, I've watched werewolves do something like that when they were mid transformation, but this was much more violent and not what I expected to see. His dark fur seemed to be shedding everywhere.

A third ring and he ran head first into one of the walls which broke his great horns, his chains fell to the ground and he was definitely shorter. Then the bell started moving of its own accord. Each time a peal rang out, more and more of Krampus' frightening exterior faded away. I mentally kept count and there were a total of twelve rings from the bell. And by the end, Krampus was no more. However a rather large old man lay in a pile of fur, horns, hooves and chains.

The corpulent geriatric rolled over to show his large white beard and balding head. His face was ruddy and looked rather jolly, however his skin was tanned as if he were from the Mediterranian Sea area. The glowing runes from the bell had finally faded and the entire necklace stilled. My mind raced with the possibility and I thought that there was no possible way it could be HIM.

I moved the bed away from my legs enough to escape and walk around to the naked man. "Um, Santa?" I asked.

He looked up at me. "Arthur, my boy! Ho ho ho! Not exactly Santa, but rather one of his counterparts, Most people call me…"

"Saint Nicholas?" asked Claud. He had aroused from his short wall induced nap to witness the transformation.

"Hold up, I thought Santa Claus and Saint Nicholas were the same person." I was genuinely confused. "And how the hell did Krampus melt into you?"

"Ho ho ho. I get this a lot. Well, for starters, Krampus and I are the same person. This is why Krampusnacht is the night before the Feast of St. Nicholas. Usually I don't go through this transformation until the 5th of December and I never attack people like I did. I just couldn't help myself. It was as if I was being controlled by someone else.

"Secondly, most countries have a different version of the spirit of giving, Santa Claus, St. Nicholas, Father Christmas, Ded Moroz, we are all different people, not one giant figure. How do you think we get those presents delivered in one night? It sure isn't one of us, but rather many of us all working together.

"Third and most important, does anyone have any clothes for me to wear?"

Claud and I chuckled at that, but quickly our chuckles died away as Tessera and Ena groaned in pain. "Oh dear, it looks like I made a mess. Let me fix this for you." Saint Nick put his finger alongside his nose and winked. All of the wounds on Tessera and Ena melted away leaving not even a reminder scar. Tria sat up and we heard the muffled thumps of Pente and Dia standing up and heading down the stairs. They surveyed the scene after helping Tria stand up and the looks of confusion on their faces were priceless.

Claud nodded at them, Ena did some kind of hand gesture as St. Nick stood up revealing his grizzled swarthy white hair and his, um… gift. "Well, I should go. Looks like I have done enough damage here," and before anyone could say or do anything, he disappeared in a puff of smoke and left nothing behind but glittering sand. To this day, I still have no idea what the fuck just happened and while I was ruminating about the sequence of events, I remembered that Forbes had slipped into the mirror a few minutes ago.

Chapter Twenty Nine

Into the Looking Glass

I quickly caught the rest of the team up on where Forbes and Allie had disappeared to at the beginning of the fracas. Pente went to the mirror and started examining it with some kind of handheld device. Ena checked out the health of the rest of the team, all of them seemed hale and strong, ready to fight again.

"Well, it looks like he used a standard transportation spell to go into the mirror," Pente started. "Its effects are lingering for some reason. Usually this kind of spell is only open for the caster and closes immediately after they step through."

I went over to the floor length mirror. I swear I heard the sound of sleigh bells and laughing. I saw a fine dusting of glittery sand. "Looks like St. Nick left us a present. Let's go." I said as I stepped in.

Claud was right behind me, but as Ena walked up to the mirror he stumbled as if pushed back. He quickly tapped it and it was solid again. "Fuck. Looks like you two are on your own, boss." Claud and I exchanged a glance. Well, I assume he was looking at me since you know, he is blind and all.

The mirrored room was exactly like the one reflected just backwards. Everything that was on the right was now on the left. It took a bit to orient ourselves, but we quickly figured it out and went after Forbes. He hadn't gotten far because the entirety of the battle with

Krampus had only taken a few minutes and we caught up with him in the bar of the club.

He tried to use the same magic as before but we knew what to look for and were able to roll out of the way. A gust of wind knocked over the tables and chairs that were between us, and Forbes again held his weird fingernail dagger to Allie's throat.

"How did you get through the mirror?" He demanded. "I knew from the moment I first heard of you and your 'services', Mr. Pax that you would be a bother to my plans. I thought I had taken care of you the first time you came into my establishment. There has not been a record of anyone remembering anything after drinking from the Lethe waters. I should have had you killed." Spittle practically flew out of his mouth in his enraged state.

Claud aimed a pistol at Forbes. "We had help from a friend."

I took the time to reach for my potions I had brewed, which somehow had survived so far. Behind my back, I poured out the vial and waited for the herbs and chemicals to mix together. I knew it would take a few seconds to work and shortly a fine mist started to roll along the ground.

I put my hands up as if surrendering. "Fine, Forbes, we are at a standstill. What do you propose?"

"Oh, my demands are simple, my boy. All of you have a drink from my Lethe spring and leave. I will not take any further action, if you just leave us alone. Rusalka and I will have a long and happy life together, whereas you will forget everything you have seen and heard here." Lethe Springs were not easy to find, but apparently he had one at his disposal. That would explain the extended hospital stay for me. Anyone drinking from the River Lethe or any of its offshoots experience swelling of the brain to the point that memories were lost. Depending on how much you consumed, was the determining factor on how much and how long your memory was gone.

"Well, you kind of have us against the ropes right now, Forbes." I smelled the lavender and valerian root starting to waft past my nose. Hopefully, it will take hold soon and we will be out of here. I just needed to keep him distracted. "Here's a counter proposal. Let my team go and I will work for you, willingly. They will not be a bother to you anymore. You have my word. With my connections, I can help make the transition much easier for the Unseelie to take control."

Forbes thought about it for a bit. Time passed slowly. We heard the sounds of footsteps from the backstage area. I thought it was the Dactyls coming through the mirror somehow, and I was partly right. A pair of guards walked in with Ena and Dei. We didn't see the other three.

"Did you dispatch the others?" Forbes asked the guards and one just nodded. "Excellent. Well, well, well Mr. Pax. looks like your little friends have met an untimely fate. I wanted to show you exactly what we do to those who stand against us. Oh, and in reference to your offer…" Forbes smiled cruelly.

"No." was all he said and flicked a look to the guards. They pulled out daggers and slit the throats of the two paratroopers they were guarding. This made Claud yell. Claud popped two shots off and both of them dropped the guards. Perfect shots to the head left small holes and silver blood running out. Forbes tightened his grip on Allie's throat and drew a small bead of blood from her neck.

Claud turned his pistol to Forbes. "Not another STEP!" Forbes yelled. His eyes looked wildly around at the scene of death around.

"None of you will leave this building alive, Pax. I promise you that. Including your precious Rusalka. If I cannot have her, no one…" he yawned. "Will. What is goin…" He slumped over on the bar, completely passed out.

Claud moved in to cuff him and remove him from the area. I rushed over to her and checked her vitals. "Are you well enough to walk, Allie?"

"Who the hell are you?" She was beyond bewildered.

"I'm Luke Skywalker and I am here to rescue you." An even more quizzical look came across her face. "Your sisters sent me to find you," I amended. She finally breathed a sigh of relief and started crying. All I could do was hold her.

Another commotion came from backstage. I was hoping it was the police and EMTs to help the glamoured workers but since we were in a mirror dimension, I had no idea who it was. There was a lot of yelling and running around. The commanding voice was a very familiar one.

Duke de Sligo came from behind the curtain wearing full battle armor and held a short sword. A handful of more battle ready Fae were right behind him. He stopped at the edge of the stage, took a sniff and covered his nose quickly smelling the sleep potion. He scanned the room and settled his gaze on the dead guards and paratroopers. Well, fuck.

"I demand to know the meaning of this intrusion! You have broken several laws of both Fae and humankind and will pay for this outrage!" The Duke looked as if he were ready to go all Conan on our asses and I just didn't have time for this horseshit.

"Hey, jackass. The only reason your boys were popped in the head is they attacked first." I felt fury starting to rise in my chest. "I get that you Fae have all your courtly drama and act like the rest of the world revolves around you, but guess what? It fucking doesn't. If I hadn't come in here to save Rusalka, the world would be put into an Ice Age it might not recover from. If it wiped out the humans, how would you survive?"

The Duke looked shocked. "What do you mean? Is this pitiful creature The Rusalka? I had no knowledge of this. I was told by the Viscount that he was only glamouring mortals."

"Did you miss the part that I spelled it all out for you last night?" I looked at Claud, "I did tell him this right or was I dreaming?"

"No, I was there with you Mr. Pax. You most certainly did tell him your intentions." Claud kept his pistol trained on the Duke.

"I have never seen either of you before in my life. Although, your reputations precede you, Mr. Pax and Dr. Cabiri. It is not often a Believer works hand in hand with a son of Hephaestus." He lowered his sword. "There is something amiss that I do not fully understand, but I will certainly get to the bottom of this."

Wait, did he say he was a son of Hephaestus? I looked at Claud. He just shrugged his shoulders. "Secrets are my life," was all he said.

With weapons put away, I detailed everything to the Duke that Forbes had divulged. De Sligo insisted he wasn't at the meeting last night, but would look into it. "The Viscount has a lot to explain," was all he said and he called for his men to go check on the other prisoners.

Thankfully, the sleep potion had dissipated enough to not affect any more of the Fae. It was fast working and left the room smelling delightful. They took their dead and disappeared.

"Viscount, if we didn't meet last night, who was I speaking with? And how do we get back to the other side of the looking glass?" I asked as we walked down the stairs filling him in on everything that had transpired this night.

"Getting you through the mirror is easy," He walked over to the glass and waived his hands. Immediately, the Dactyls came pouring through the portal.

"The fuck?" both Claud and I asked.

"But we watched them kill you two," I pointed at Ena and Dia. The Viscount shook his head.

"It must have been a glamour. There are many questions that Forbes will have to answer for." He walked through the mirror along with the rest of his guards and Forbes. We quickly joined them before the mirror portal shut again.

A quick call to my police contacts and the ambulances were on the way to take care of the glamoured humans forced to work there every night. The people were sore and tired, but relatively healthy. Forbes was arrested and taken away with a sleepy snarl. The Dactyls, Claud, Allie and I were checked out and released on the scene. The only thing left was getting Allie home and figuring out what the actual fuck had just happened.

Chapter Thirty
All's Well and Stuff

Over the next few days, reunions and bittersweet tears happened. I formally requested an audience with the Duke, only to be turned down. He had already left the country. From what I gathered, he was looking for a new Viscount of Indiana already, but the Fae kept their secrets close to themselves. Just like Claud.

We had a nice long chat about his ancestry and his strike force. They were apparently some of his brothers, the Cabiri, a demigod race that was sired by the great Greek forger himself. I should have known better, I mean Claud translated from Greek means 'lame' and the Cabiri were a lesser known demi-god that was worshipped in small areas around the Greek countryside.

"Wait, so you're telling me that the Greek gods are real? I was taught that most of the myths were just that, myths." I reeled from the revelation.

"There is a lot that the Believers are not told, Mr. Pax. There are many pathways to reach enlightenment and the sect called the Believers are one of many." Claud had a slight smile on his face. That bastard.

"You know, you can call me Artie. I mean after everything we've been through we can cut through the formalities." He nodded.

"As you wish, Mr. Pax." I just cannot with this guy. My phone buzzed with a text from Danni. It had been a few days since we rescued her sister and I was giving them some time to have a proper reunion. She invited us over for dinner to discuss things. I had hoped this wasn't the beginning of a Dear John letter.

Claud drove us over to their house which was already decorated for Christmas, even though Thanksgiving hadn't happened yet. I guess in lieu of the current circumstances, exceptions can be made. He parked and just went in the door. Not even opening my door or anything. I mean, contractually, he was finished being my driver slash bodyguard slash doctor, but I had gotten used to him opening my door. A demigod, opening my door. What a wicked twist.

I walked up the path and steps to the house and before I could reach the handle, the door opened. Danni looked spectacular in the green velvet dress she was wearing. She wrapped me in a hug that melted me from head to toe. "Heya, stranger." she breathed into my ear. Our lips met and our passion exploded. I'm sure the door was closed, because I didn't feel the chill of the wind behind me anymore. God I was hoping this didn't turn into a Dear John moment.

"Ahem," a voice came from behind Danni and we broke our embrace, just slightly embarrassed. I looked up to see the rest of the sisters, including whom I could only assume was Sonya, since I had never seen her before in person.

"Um, yeah. Ah. Hi?" I stammered, which caused the sisters, including Rochelle to giggle. They in turn all gave me hugs of thanks ending with Allie, who looked in perfect health. Danni took my hand and led me into the family room.

"Artie, I wanted to introduce you to the rest of the family." Fuck, I feel like I was being ambushed. I looked in the room and there was Claud talking to two older gentlemen. One with a long grey beard and one a long white beard. "These are my Uncles, Vasha and Yuri." The memory of the dream kicked in. I had seen these two before, they were saving my ass from the legion of souls. They both came over to me with back slaps and cheers of appreciation for saving their niece. The next thing I knew, a shot glass was forced into my hand.

"A TOAST!" shouted Vasha in a thick Russian accent. "You have saved our family and the world from another Ice Age. May your life be long and the sun always shine bright! As bright as your future!" We all knocked back the clear liquid, which happened to be the finest tasting vodka I had ever had the pleasure of drinking. There was no burn or bad aftertaste. The glass was quickly replaced with a darker liquid.

"A TOAST!' shouted Yuri in an even thicker Russian accent. "You have tamed our wild niece, Danni with the fiery passion of your love. May your nights be full of wonder and exotic joys." I visibly blushed at that and everyone laughed at my expense and we knocked back the most vile concoction I had ever had the displeasure of tasting. It tasted like medicine, prunes and burning. I looked at the rest of the party and no one else had sipped the dark brew.

"What the hell was that?" I coughed and everyone else laughed again at my expense.

Yuri, looking like an impish Santa Claus, took the glass from my hand. "In Belorus, it is a tincture called balsam. It is for your health and wellness. And for our enjoyment." He let out a full belly laugh that would put any mall Santa to shame.

"Thanks, I think?" I sputtered out. I needed another drink to get this foul taste out of my mouth. "I have a question. Recently, I had a dream that had the two of you starring in it. There were carts and souls escaping and a red beam of light. I know pretty much everyone else in here's alter ego. Do you mind if I ask who you are?"

Yuri and Vasha exchanged a meaningful look. Rochelle took the glass from my hand and replaced it with what looked like a proper Gin and Tonic. "Oh, come, now, Mr. Pax. Now is not the time to discuss work, now is the time for celebrating. I have already had the funds transferred to your account to take care of the business portion of our agreement. Tonight though, we celebrate our found sister and the return of the natural order of things. Tomorrow, we can deal with the details."

"Tomorrow? Wait what day is tomorrow?" I picked up my phone and looked at the date. "Oh crap. Aunt Shirley…" Quizzical looks went back and forth like a tennis match, but the uncles just started laughing again as we all went into the formal dining room with a beautifully prepared feast in front of us. Danni made sure to sit next to me and tease me under the table. Tonight I wouldn't worry about dealing with the Graces and just enjoy the company I had.

Outside I heard the croaking of two ravens as they took wing from one of the barren trees. There were a lot of unanswered questions, but that was for another day.

Epilogue

The smell of the fresh rain came wafting in through the windows. It had been a harsh winter for everyone, but especially in November. Parts of the world that normally didn't get snow had experienced its first taste since the Ice Age. Normally hearty plants that thrived in tropical climates, felt the bitter chill of Jack Frost's breath. Fortunately, it hadn't lasted very long, just enough to cause a stir and then it was gone again.

The owner of the window knew that spring was on its way finally because she had read the signs. The mice that scurried through her small house were extremely active at the smell of the upcoming rain. Her birds she kept covered during the night were getting restless, so the occupant went to remove the dark fabric. The finches burst forth with a joyous song as she opened the cage to let them out for a bit. She only let them fly around the house in the winter, because it would help keep them warm.

The small flock of finches flittered here and there amongst the dried herbs and living plants she kept in her house. If one looked around, they could easily identify cooking herbs like rosemary, thyme, sage and oregano. Upon a closer inspection, they could see more nefarious plants, like mugwort, nightshade and deadly toadstools.

She always had heat in the fireplace. Right now, it was starting to die down, so she grabbed a couple more logs and put them on. Instantly, they caught fire and burst red and warm again. The finches twittered and chirped out of appreciation in the rafters of the simple wooden cottage, removed far from the city.

It was a simple life for the lonely woman, but she was satisfied. She bustled about gathering up ingredients for a light lunch. Cheese, hard boiled eggs and the last scrap of bread. She nodded because she knew she needed to make a trip into town to buy more flour, but not right now. Now was the time to relax, enjoy the song of her finches and eat a simple meal.

As she went to sit, a knock on the door startled her. The birds fell silent. With a groan, she put her meal down and went to the front door. She wasn't expecting company today, but she rarely expected anyone to make the trek out to her cottage.

Another thump. "I'm coming. I'm coming," she griped and opened the door. Outside shivering in the still chilly air was a young lady. "What'cher need?" the lady asked.

The girl looked in her eyes and opened her coat. Her belly was round with child and her face said it all. The more matronly woman ushered her in out of the cold. "Have a seat by the fire and tell me all about it, child."

The girl burst into tears and told a tale about a rich boy and having his way with her. She was ashamed to go to the hospital and get the unwanted pregnancy taken care of. She had hid it from her parents and friends and had heard about the services the matron had to offer.

"Child, you are too far along for what I could have offered you if you had come straight here," the matron looked at the heart stricken youth. "I will give you the services of a midwife, if you help me around the house. If you want to give the child up for adoption, I know where we can take it."

"No, Baba, you misunderstand." the young maiden said. "I fully intend to keep this child. I want your help getting rid of the bastard that did this to me."

The older lady smiled a twisted and wicked smile. She stood silently, went over to her bookshelf and removed a book that was covered in an oiled, canvas cloth. "You are still welcome to live here after, I am in need of an apprentice and I can tell you are just the help I have been looking for."

She removed the cloth and an ancient leather bound tome opened up to reveal strange symbols, intricate drawings of plants and animal anatomies. Secrets passed down from one generation to the next of the inner workings of all life on Earth and beyond lay in that book. It seemed to never end as the pages flipped rapidly by themselves as if driven by a wind that neither of the women felt. The birds started chirping and screaming at each other again dancing among the eaves of the humble house. The fire blazed brighter and hotter than before.

„What is your name, child?" The older woman squinted at her new charge.

"Diana Pax."

A look of shock came across the face of the wyld woman. "Let us begin."

Bonus Short Story

The Tale of the Lusty, Busty Librarian

It was a few months into my sophomore year and I was working on the final research project for my newest history class, Intro to Historical Documents. We were assigned to find one primary source, a document that was originally written like the Magna Carta or Martin Luther's 95 Theses, and write a short essay on the style of writing, the content and conjecture on the author's original meaning and intent. By short essay, the processor meant at least one thousand words.

October was about midway through the semester and I really wanted to get a good start on it before the Fall break, which is typically around the American Thanksgiving holiday. I also wanted a good start on it before my birthday week, which led up to Fall break. Personally, I despise the term Fall for the name of the season because the name was coined in the seventeenth century due to the leaves falling from the trees. Most of the rest of the world calls the season between summer and winter, Autumn after the Latin word, autumnus, meaning "the passing of the year." In my humble opinion, I find calling the season Autumn more poetic and more correct than Fall for "leaf fall from tree."

Thus it was a few weeks before Autumn break and a few days before All Hallowed Saints Day Eve, better known as Halloween. Yes there were parties I could go to, yes there were better ways to spend a Friday night almost a fortnight before I turned 20, but there I was, in the library. Studying. At least it was quiet in the stacks tonight.

I was searching the card catalogue for ideas on which document I wanted to read, as you do. I know a lot of the students were using the campus computers to search the internet, but waiting for it to dial up just took too long for me. I had a great relationship with Mr. Dewey's system and didn't feel the need to use something as unreliable as the internet. I had a difficult enough time using the word processors to type up my papers to have them printed out. I really loved using my grandfather's typewriter, but the professors insisted that we learned to use the computers. They were also working on updating all the IBM computers to have a program called Windows 95, but it was a slow process and one I wanted nothing to do with it.

Indiana University the cutting edge of technology. Seriously, just give me a card catalogue and the direction to the stacks.

I was tracking down a particularly interesting work written by King James VI and I of Scotland and England, respectively. You know, the guy who had the Bible retranslated? Apparently, he was also a bit of an occultophile. He wrote a series of books fully titled, *Daemonologie, In Forme of a Dialogue, Divided into three Books: By the High and Mighty Prince, James by the Grace of God King of England, Scotland, France and Ireland Defender of the Faith, &c.,* more commonly known as Demonology.

I had spoken with my professor as soon as I first heard about the works and he wanted me to search it out, but focus on one part of it, rather than the entirety of the work. That's what my mission was on this evening.

Demonology was broken down into three parts and a separate pamphlet, which was published in London in 1591, titled *Newes from Scotland - declaring the damnable life and death of Dr. Fian, a notable sorcerer.* It spoke about the North Berwick witch trial in which testimonies were given directly to King James VI and I and condemned a particularly infamous woman named Geillis Duncan. Little did I know this was to be the first step on a long trail that would lead me to Salem in 1692.

I found the appropriate card file in the catalogue and being a responsible student, I wrote down the information in my notebook to track down the book. It didn't take me long to search and find the correct section in the library. I was very familiar already with the twists and turns of the Herman B Wells Library and had only gotten lost a few times in my freshman year.

I passed by one of the windows and saw the sliver of the growing moon swing its Cheshire Cat grin at me as I neared the correct section as if inviting me to come out and enjoy the revelries happening all over the campus and surrounding neighborhoods. I will admit to being tempted, because the chill of the night air and the crunch of the fallen leaves always gave me a thrill. Alas, I was determined to find this tome.

Narrowing down a new book in the depths of the library also gave me a thrill. I found the stack, section and shelf it was on and found an empty hole where the library's only copy resided. A little confused and miffed, I searched the surrounding shelves to see if it was misplaced, but came up empty. I groaned in frustration because it meant that I had to go to the one place I despised in the library, the reference desk.

I am a very self sufficient individual and pride myself on being able to find most anything in the library, however, sometimes even I come up empty handed and have to go seek the help of professionals. The one in particular I had to go speak to was the aged, lemon faced Ms. Crumblebutt. I wish I had made up her name, but that is what she was given in life.

Not much was known about Importance Crumblebutt, known as Portance, other than she never married and devoted her life to the pursuit of scholarly tome shelving and the cessation of students from snogging in the stacks. She was a solid woman of girth and slight of height, roughly five feet tall by five feet wide and as far as anyone knows has never smiled in the entire fifty years she worked at this particular library. It is rumored she is a direct descendant of the Crumblebutt family that came over on the Mayflower and still holds true to her Puritan heritage.

I sighed, squared up my shoulders and headed back down the seven flights of stairs it took to get to the information desk. On my way down, I ran through several scenarios on how to interact with Ol' Lemonface, but I knew from experience, you had to expect the unexpected. I was also slightly worried she might remember me from the first week of Freshman year, when I tried to reserve a group study room for myself because I had so many books I wanted to read through. She didn't take kindly to my "gross abuse of resources."

Rounding the corner to the desk, I saw it was empty. I knew that there was an old timey push bell to ring if she wasn't there. "Push once and wait," were the instructions listed on a neatly handwritten sign in front of the bell, which I did. I witnessed one of the lunk headed jocks ring the bell three times. I've never seen Ms. Crumblebutt whip around a corner and power walk as fast as I did that day. He was reaching out to ring a fourth time and out of nowhere a wooden ruler appeared in her hand to rap his knuckles, one hit for each ring. In a very quiet but menacing voice she reminded him that he "...needed to ring once for service."

I've never seen so many people look like they just had their knuckles rapped as if they all felt the sting of that particular ruler before.

I heard footsteps coming from the office area fully expecting Crumblebutt to come around the corner, but for some reason the gait and rap of the shoes were off. I had spent many late nights here in the library and knew Crumblebutt's walk just by sound. She preferred to work late nights because only the most studious of patrons were usually here, or the horniest. There were plenty of nooks and crannies in the library to have "study sessions" and she knew each and every one. I swear Crumblebutt must be part fae because she could sneak up on each and every one, if she was inclined to.

The click tap of shoes rounded the corner and before me was something I thought I would never see in my entire life, a different person working the evening shift. She stood about the same height as Crumblebutt, but was wildly different in appearance. She had dark brown, almost black hair, that framed her lightly olive skinned oval face with soft curls. Her dark eyes sparkled with intelligence and mischief that matched her full red stained lips. Shaped like a well put together cello, her curves and lines flowed while playing a seductive melody that was her natural walk. She wore a simple white blouse and grey skirt that both accentuated her curves and looked professional. She was carrying a small stack of books in her arms that seemed to push up her ample cleavage.

My heart and jaw dropped. I had never seen someone as well put together as this Rubenesque stranger coming towards me with a tick tap of each quick step. And the calves that were straining to keep her aloft over the two inch heels that beat out her cadence. My heart immediately picked up the pace of her walk and accelerated past it.

My mind was reeling with having to stammer out my request. *Play it cool. Be suave. You've honey spoken to plenty of college girls. You've got this. Just ask for the book and move on.*

And, yet when she came up to the desk and put the stack of books down, her ruby lips parted and out came the most seductive thing I have ever heard a woman speak, "How may I service you tonight?"

It might have been the words themselves or the soft Spanish accent she spoke with, but my mind went blank. I tried to make my mouth work. I tried to get my eyes to look anywhere else but in her deep brown eyes. I felt my face flush and tried to turn tail and run back to the stacks like a frightened mouse, but I was transfixed.

Several heartbeats passed without any sound except my heartbeat pulsing in my ears and our breathing. Her breathing quickened by the pace she was walking to get to the desk, my breath quickened by watching her walk to get to the desk. Ol' Crumblebutt never walked quickly to get anywhere. She had the slow creepy stealth of a horror movie villain.

"Are you alright?" the vision asked. I somehow found the ability to nod my head and lift my arm to present the sheet of paper with the call number on it.

"Not on shelf," I stammered out. "You pretty..." THE FUCK DID I JUST SAY? "...new. You're pretty new to the library." I recovered. My face must be cooked lobster red right now quickly going to purple from embarrassment. The heartbeat in my ears was almost the only thing I heard, my vision started to swim. She giggled.

The sound of her deep throaty giggle helped pull me away from passing out entirely, as if she had magic in her vocal cords. "Si. I am new to the library. I am filling in on evenings for Importance." The way she pronounced Crumblebutt's first name placed the accent on the third syllable and added an Espaniole flair to the last syllable, like im-por-TAN-say. I had never heard a word more seductive in my short life.

She looked at the call number for the book and gasped a little. "Oh, you are studying witches, no? It just so happens I have the book you are looking for. I was wanting to do a little light reading myself tonight." She was practically purring by the end of her statement and I was practically in love.

She shuffled through the stack of books she was carrying. I caught a few of the titles, *Malleus Malefacarum, Cases of Consciousness, A Study of Salem* and even a book about St. Augustine of Hippo.

"Ah. Here it is," She smiled brightly and started to hand it over, but pulled it back. "You are not one of those witch hunters, no? I'd hate to have to fight against such a fine young man," she laughed again and I was completely confused by her statement. Was she calling herself a witch? My face must have given away my thoughts because she laughed even harder which rippled nicely throughout her entire body.

"Oh, you poor frightened little puppy, I meant because I was dressing up as a witch for Halloween. Ai, dios mi, I forgot my hat, I'd forget my head if it weren't attached." She jibed at me and pulled out the classic black pointed witch hat from under the desk and placed it rakishly on her head. I don't know how she did it, but the hat made her go from sultry to downright adorable.

I gulped and stammered out a negative sound, which made her tinkle out a sultry laugh again as she handed me the book. I cast my eyes down to the book and fumbled out a thank you.

"You are welcome, mi corderito asustado." She invitingly replied. "Just make sure you bring me the book back. It's going to be a lonely night for me. Unless you want to keep me company?" And there it was. I went full purple and quickly turned to beat a hasty retreat.

Before I could walk away, I felt her well manicured hand on my shoulder. I turned my head a bit to catch her eyes. "My name is Elisheba, if you have any questions."

I finally worked up the courage to speak. "Isn't that the Hebrew form on Isabella? By your accent I assumed you were of some Spanish origin." I turned back to her.

"Si. You are learned as well as handsome. You are correct on both parts. I am Spanish, but also Jewish. My family lived in Ceuta, Spain for generations, even during the Spanish Inquisition. We have roots that go all the way back to Jerusalem and have kept the traditions of our ancestors, even if it was in secret." She was spellbinding as she spoke about her family. I listened to her explain her family history for over an hour, asking questions to clarify spots here and there. The best part was she was only five years older than me, working on her Doctorate in Library Sciences.

We spoke off and on for the rest of the evening, swapping stories and just generally enjoying ourselves as the time slipped away stealthily. It didn't occur to me that no one else was in the library until it was time to close up. I checked out the book for reading later with the promise that I would return it to her directly. I bid Elisheba a fond goodnight and left, my head swimming with the possibilities of having more stimulating, um, "conversations" with her.

It was a couple weeks before I could get back to the library again, with all the parties that My Friend Chuck ™ continuously dragged me to and the other assignments I had to work on before break. I had told Chuck and other friends about her to see if I was crazy or not. Turns out I was crazy because NO ONE had seen her. Ms. Crumblebutt was the evening librarian and the head of the dept, Dr. McEntyre was the day librarian.

Like I said it was a couple of weeks before I went back and steeled up my nerve to go and return the book, only to find Crumblebutt on the counter. I made inquiries about Elisheba and she acted like I had grown a second head. She insisted that the library was closed that entire weekend and they had been looking for that particular book for a few weeks and how dare I take a reference book out of the library. I swear I saw her reaching for the ruler, but Dr. McEntyre came around the corner from the office to see what the commotion was all about. I explained to him what had happened a fortnight ago and he was just as confused as Crumblebutt and insisted that the library was closed all weekend due to the holiday and past pranks that had been played around the Devil's Night. He very politely thanked me for returning such a valuable book and reminded me that reference books were to remain in the library, although copies could be made for a small fee that could be charged to my student account.

I was thoroughly confused and very chastised as I turned to walk back out the door. I'm sure Crumblebutt was visually throwing dagger sharpened rulers at my back. I did notice out of the corner of my eye a rather pretty faced student walking in, she was wearing thick black glasses, an IU ball cap and a rather comfy looking pair of sweats, but it was the eyes that caught my attention. They twinkled with intelligence and mischief, but she was gone around a corner before my brain caught up with my gaze and I dismissed it.

I felt as if I would never see my Lusty Busty Librarian again, but that night has come to the forefront of my thoughts many times the rest of the semester. After coming back from Christmas break, I returned to the library after rumors of a new librarian because Crumblebutt finally retired. Which was odd because it was the middle of the school year. In the whispers of my fellow students, I had learned enough to form my opinion, that it must be my LBL. I went in with a grin and saw the soft brown curls framing the familiar face of Elisheba. She looked up from her reading and returned my smile.

"You are very late returning my book to me. I believe a punishment is in order, Mr. Pax." She reached for the ruler and I had flashbacks to Crumblebutt. Just as she picked it up she broke out in tittering laughter that shook her well formed frame.

She was the evening librarian for a semester because of issues with people constantly hitting on her and asking her out, which she stood fast and refused because she was a professional, after all. I tried to remain in contact with her but over the years she has disappeared from the public eye. I never learned her last name, which was my fault, but I remain hopeful that someday I will see my LBL Elisheba again.

Author's Note:

Greetings and well met, Believers. If you have made it this far, you deserve a bit of an explanation. What a wild ride this experience has been. I have always wanted to write a book, although I never knew what it was going to be about. One wintery day, an inspiration hit me. But, before we get there, I should explain a few things first.

I was born in Arkansas, but my family moved up to Indianapolis when I was still a baby. People say write what you know, so I did. I lived in Indianapolis until my early twenties. By the time I moved away, I had already been married once and fathered two children.

While living there, I visited many of the places mentioned in the story: Garfield Park and the Marion County Library main branch were two places I practically lived in. I lived on the south side of town, a stone's throw away from Fountain Square, with my parents and my four siblings. I never realized it until I revisited the old stomping grounds, but we always had the biggest house on the block. I guess when you have seven adults and several cats you need a big place.

It was my third grade year that I discovered Tolkien and Bulfinch's Mythology. Those led me to finding out there were more wonderful worlds to discover in the words of the past. I fell in love with cryptozoology and folktales. Before the library was renovated to the towering glass behemoth it is now, I knew exactly where to find the folktales and mythology, and I would gather as many books as my allotment allowed. Well, I also grabbed comic strip books, like Garfield and Calvin and Hobbes.

My obsession was put on the back burner as I grew and started a family, but it was always there. Fast forward to the summer of 1999. My Aunt Alma was working at this place for several summers, a place called the Ohio Renaissance Festival. It was after my first marriage had dissolved and a couple of other failed relationships that I auditioned and was accepted as a street cast member as a washing wench. I know, usually the term wench is reserved for the female persuasion, however this was not the case with me. I was stationed at the washing well with other wenches and that started my love for all things Renfaire.

It was that year I wooed a young lady and we were wed the next year. It didn't last as long as I would have liked, but every relationship is a learning tool. From there, I went on the road and eventually landed in Arizona. The next decade or so of my life was spent out there. (Don't worry you will get Arizona stuff in the next book.)

While in Arizona, I rekindled my love for stage acting, met both of my partners, started my collegiate career, and volunteered at the local comic convention. It was there that I started running panels for folklore, monsters, and mythology, thus getting me back to my passion. There was also a lot of music, but that's another story.

My wife, Amy, and I never really settled on the idea of being monogamous, and eventually we met our partner, Stacia. (Ooh, watch out he's one of those polyamorous thruple weirdos!) Then the Autumn of 2019 changed our lives forever. Stacia had been offered a position in North Carolina with one of the leading forklift companies in the world. The three of us talked about the possibility for a long time before we made a final decision. We were moving out to North Carolina. Well, part of us moved. At first it was just Stacia and me, leaving Amy with the youngest two kids. We were all supposed to move out here together after the school year let out, but the Coronavirus happened. I'll get to that in a minute.

When we moved out to NC, we didn't exactly have a place lined up to live, but a coworker graciously offered up their beach house until we were able to get a rental of our own. Holy wow, that was awesome. The only part that wasn't awesome was the two-hour one-way drive to her work every day. We were glad when we found a place closer.

It was on one of those drives in the winter months, that I saw steam rising up from a pond as the sun's rays lit upon the surface. An idea lept to my brain, "What if those were the souls of departed people trying to get back to this plane?" That thought is what started this story. I had many drafts originally, but nothing quite worked. Then one day, my fingers started flowing and the word of Arthur Pax came to be.

Back to the story. Stacia and I were safe in our cute little rental, but Amy and the kids still had contractual obligations to work at the Arizona Renaissance Festival, which was running at the beginning of the outbreak. I had plans to drive back to Arizona and collect the family to move them all out here. Then the worst possible thing happened. Amy tested positive for Covid-19. We aren't sure how it happened, because we were taking all the correct precautionary measures. The only thing we could piece together is it happened on my drive or at the grocery store. We were all terrified it would end badly because she has a laundry list of health issues.

I stayed there with her during this time and we made a plan to move everyone when she was healthier. Then, Stacia's health took a turn for the worse. Thankfully this time it wasn't Covid related; still not good, but not Covid. We made the decision to move the youngest child to North Carolina so I could return to NC.

The book only took me a couple months to get written before edits and rewrites. Thankfully, my Aunt Alma came to the rescue again and introduced me to the publishing house that helped me finish my goal of creating this book.

For those of you wondering, yes, the history written in the book was not only researched by me, but I also lived it in some ways. There is a lot of me that is manifested in Arthur Pax, but Arthur is still his own entity and I am simply telling his story. This is just the beginning of a series of books. I am excited to find out more about his life, his lineage, and his future.

Until next time, keep Believing and keep dreaming. You never know what you are capable of until you attempt to do something.

Acknowledgements:

There are many people that have helped me during this process that I would like to recognize: Amy and Stacia, my Otters, have been great at being a sounding board for my ideas. My Beta Readers Club offered tips and caught small things I missed the first five times I read through the book. My parents have always been there supporting my next crazy idea.

To my children: If I could tell you two things in life, they would be, 1) You never know what you can do until you try, and 2) having separate blankets is a key component to a successful relationship.

www.ingramcontent.com/pod-product-compliance
Lightning Source LLC
Chambersburg PA
CBHW060559310726
48982CB00008B/1170/J